# Metamorphosis of Memphis
## The Blues and Beale Street, 1819-2019

**On the front cover:**

The Hernando de Soto Bridge
(Opened, August 2, 1973)

Lemuel Colbert-Chickasaw

Andrew Jackson, John Overton

Robertson Topp, James Winchester, Ida B. Wells

Robert R. Church, Sr., W. C. Handy, Lt. George Lee

Furry Lewis, Wanda Newborn, Evelyn Young, B. B. King

[Foundational individuals to the legacy of
Memphis, the Blues and Beale Street]

# Metamorphosis of Memphis

## The Blues and Beale Street
## 1819 - 2019

By

## Dr. L. LaSimba M. Gray, Jr.

**Metamorphosis of Memphis**
Copyright © 2025



Updated Editing/Revisions: Pamela D. Cox (PCox Enterprises)
Cover Design by Angelique M. Gray

ISBN: 9798998624728 (Paperback)
ISBN: 9798998624711 (EBook)

Printed in the United States of America

# Table of Contents

# DEDICATION

In writing this book, I had cause to look back over my childhood and to walk down memory lane. This memory lane was that of my early childhood, my adolescence, my high school and college years, and the wonderful life I have lived in Memphis as an adult. I will tell all my friends, "Whenever I leave Memphis, I always get a round-trip ticket!" I stand in awe of the miraculous manner in which my God-fearing parents raised me. With tremendous love and caring discipline, they provided the necessities of life for me, and most admirable of all, they skillfully protected me while growing up in a completely segregated society. I became acutely aware of and now truly recognize and appreciate the power of the 'village.' The village of neighbors chipped in to help shape my vision of and for life.

*Leo and Corine Gray,
the author's parents.*

I remember when the wading pool in Winchester Park on High and Lane Street was opened to the public, but for Whites only. Every child always wants to get into the water where there is a wading pool. But sadly, all I could do was watch as the White children came in droves wearing their bathing suits with their long, lush and beautiful beach towels.

Thanks to the compassion and love for children displayed by a neighbor, Mrs. Cleo Dickens, who, seeing the hurtfulness of alienation in our eyes as one who understood that alienation and as one who had also felt the pain of rejection, would then holler out, "all right children get your shorts on and let's have some fun!" She would turn on her water hose and sprinkle us with cool water for hours at a time. When her arms became tired of holding the water hose up, she would call me saying, "Big Boy, you come and sprinkle some; now, don't get the girls' hair wet!" (Big Boy was my childhood nickname). Of course, being a youngster, that was like telling me to wet the girl's hair. Every time I caught her not watching me, I sprayed the girls with water right on their heads, making sure I got their hair wet. To my delight, the girls would scream, "Ms. Dickens, Big Boy wet my hair!" I would double over in laughter as I watched the girls screaming and trying to rid their hair of the water.

I am and shall always be eternally grateful to my father, the late Reverend Leo M. Gray, Sr., for his presence and involvement in the growth and development of me and my siblings. We never ate a meal in the Gray house without my father saying grace over that meal. We never went to bed without my father being home at night. My mother, the late Corine Olivia Gray, was my first teacher. We did not have Pre-K at Grant School in 1952, but when the Gray children reported to first grade, we all knew our ABC's and we could count. We knew our address and telephone number (a party line). Mom taught us our Easter speeches and insisted on us memorizing the entire speech.

Mom was my first doctor; she knew how to bandage cuts. She knew how to release pressure from punctured, swollen feet. She knew how to mix kerosene and sugar for coughs. She knew how to pour castor oil. At night, when she finished 'doctoring' on us, she would give us a hug and say, "Go to sleep." For me, however, when she doctored on me, oh, what tenderness when she doctored on me, it felt as though all of her love was showered on me. After she doctored on me, she would give me a big hug and say softly, "Now go to sleep, Big Boy."

In keeping with our strong family ties, without my siblings, I do not know where I would be today. My siblings were always there in times of need, all seven of them: Maxine, Nacolis, Bobby, my twin Cleo, Roberta, Vernita, and Ruth Denise. Maxine was my protector; she would literally fight for me. Nacolis was always tearing our toys into seemingly hundreds of pieces, and then he would put them back together. Bobbie was our pace setter. She was a straight-A student and the first to go to college. She attended Tougaloo Christian College in Jackson, Mississippi. She returned to Memphis in 1964 and became a teacher at Prospect Elementary. Bobbie paid for my room and board at Lane College from 1964-1966.

Maxine attended LeMoyne-Owen College. Growing up, she would finish eating dinner and would immediately go to bed. Over in the night while the rest of us slept, she would go to the kitchen and transform Momma's kitchen into her study hall. She would have her books spread out all over the kitchen table to study. It became readily apparent to me as to when one could study successfully in a house of ten people.

Cleo enrolled in the Memphis Art Academy, as he was gifted with great artistic ability. He was drafted and joined the United States Air Force. It was my job to look after Nacolis, Roberta, Vernita, and Ruth Denise. Nacolis started independent living at an early age. He got a job, rented an apartment, and had a closet filled with sharp, slick suits that I could borrow for special events at Lane College.

Bobbie and Maxine were very accomplished teachers in the Memphis City School System and taught for 30-plus years. Roberta finished LeMoyne-Owen College, then Meharry Medical College, and went on to a career practicing medicine. Vernita and Ruth attended Spelman College in Atlanta, Georgia. Vernita majored in Pre-Med and graduated from Meharry Medical College and became a medical doctor. Ruth took on a double major in Mathematics and Electrical Engineering and went into the corporate world. Georgia Tech and Spelman collaborated to develop a program to attract and produce more African American Engineers. I, as you have probably already surmised, am extremely proud of all seven of my sisters and brothers!

We were so fortunate to have been born into a blessed and loving home with God-fearing parents. We were blessed to have lived in progressively powerful and family-oriented neighborhoods. I remember and appreciate the odd jobs neighbors would give the boys, such as raking leaves, sweeping yards, and going to the corner grocery to buy their cokes and goodies. These jobs helped tremendously in building our character and laying the groundwork for building a strong work ethic. I am eternally grateful to all of those who were instrumental in helping us develop this work ethic that has carried many of us on throughout our lives. I ask God's blessings on the memories of these persons as well as blessings on the descendants of these great people.

Therefore, in great appreciation and tender reverence for all of the above and for so, much, much more, I humbly dedicate this book to my parents, my siblings, the elders of High Street, the elders of Ralston Avenue, the elders of Silver Street, and the elders of Jagoe, Mississippi.

# PREFACE - I


**By**

**Jimmy Ogle**

**Former Shelby County Historian**


Memphis is located on the highest piece of ground on the Mississippi River between Cairo, Illinois, and Natchez, Mississippi. This fourth Chickasaw Bluff on the east bank of the Mississippi River in West Tennessee is literally the high dry ground that centuries ago served as a safe and dry place for animals to keep their paws dry. Native Americans followed the animal trails in the last two thousand years, then the European explorers, and then American settlers by the early nineteenth century.

The soils of the Mid-South area and the Delta have annually been replenished by the fluctuation of the Mississippi River. This led to the 19th century development of an agrarian culture of hardwood and cotton, and then in the 20th century, with the advent of modern transportation of "river, railways, roadways, and runways."

Memphis was the northern capital of the Delta – the business, banking, shopping, cultural, social, medical, and transportation center.

In the 1990s, when the National Museum of American History of the Smithsonian Institution wrote its story "Rock 'n' Soul: Social Crossroads," the most telling statement was "in the quest to identify the roots of America's music, all roads led to Memphis."

The story of the spirituals, work songs, and field hollers was an expression that rose from the hardships of working these fields for a living, a meager living. These expressions became gospel, country, and blues that were brought northward up the Blues Highway (U.S. 61) during the out-migration of former slaves and sharecroppers, the 19th and 20th centuries, to urban centers such as Memphis, St. Louis, Chicago, and Detroit, seeking economic opportunity and hope.

"The Blues are the roots, and the rest are the fruits," according to blues legend Willie Dixon. In Memphis, the "original American musical art form" – the Blues was allowed to flourish on Beale Street, then the African American population center. In the first half of the 20th century, Beale Street was a mile of "vice and commercial ambition; owned by the Jews, policed by the whites and enjoyed by the Negroes" according to Lt. George W. Lee, the unofficial "Mayor of Beale Street." W.C. Handy was the first to publish a blues song in America (The Memphis Blues) from his offices on Beale Street in 1912.

At that time, Memphis was a hard town, leading the nation in crime, murder, drugs, vice, and gambling – all under a strict political "white" rule. During these hard times of Jim Crow and segregation (and "separate but equal" – that was not equal), whites were allowed to go to Beale Street, but blacks were not allowed on Main Street. And those curious whites were drawn to that raw, gutsy sound and action on Beale Street. From this sound and creativity sprang rock 'n' roll (at Sun Studio) and soul (at Stax). And the rest is history . . .

Memphis is the "Home of the Blues, Birthplace of Rock 'n' Roll, Cradle of Soul, and Crossroads of American Music" with Handy Park being at the Crossroads of America's Music, at the intersection of B.B. King Blvd. and Beale Street!

Dr. LaSimba Gray, Jr. has been able to place this history into a context through study, deliberation, interviews, and his own testimony and life experiences in the Delta, in Memphis, and during the past seventy years of massive changes in Memphis when crossing over from the 20th century into the 21st century. Both behind the scenes and out front, he was there.

He covers the influences on Memphis starting with the life and achievements of Robert Church, Sr., the Reconstruction Era, Yellow Fever devastation, Immigration from the Delta and Immigration from Europe,

Progressive Era, Raring 20s, Politic, Bossism, World War 2, Corporate Agricultural influences, Civil Rights and Desegregation – being able to "live the life" of metamorphosis and transformation, seeing the struggles through the eyes of a Pastor, Community Leader and Activist – through a prism like no other. Being willing to put all this on paper for the world to see and read is a brave moment for him, and we are all the better for it.

Jimmy Ogle
Former Shelby County Historian

# PREFACE - II

**By**

**Lucy Yates Shaw Henderson**

**Former Chairman, Board of Directors, Tri-State Bank**

## "Being on Beale Street"

I was pretty much raised on Beale and Third Street, as well as our home house between Vance and Linden on Cynthia Place. I went to Leath Elementary on Linden, which was just across the street from Church Park and Turley Drive, with a path that led directly to Beale Street. My parents, John and Sadie Yates had seven children, and all but one attended Leath Elementary.

My parents owned rooming houses on Cynthia, apartments right behind the fire station at Linden and Beale Street, and a hotel and café (Yates Hotel and Good Eats Café) three doors down from Beale on Third Street. My parents were very motivated entrepreneurs and successful in ways that few "colored people" could be who were without more than an 8th grade education or a preacher. However, they were both ahead of their time—aggressive, with an uncanny understanding of money, business, and how to treat others with dignity and respect.

The café was established right next door to Lipsey's Fish Market on Third Street. There was never a time that fried buffalo fish, that melted in your mouth, was not on our menu. My Daddy used to pay my eldest brothers to clean chitterlings out back. They soon preferred working at the South Memphis icehouse over cleaning chitterlings! In fact, they had paper routes, worked at the bowling alleys, setting up pins and anything to avoid working in the kitchen! Our business was booming because the hotel and café slept and fed black folk who came to Memphis from the rural parts of Mississippi and Arkansas on the weekends to shop on Beale Street, go to a movie (The Old and the New Daisy), get dry goods and church supplies from A. Schwab, go to the King's Palace Juke Joint for fun or maybe they came to visit a Pentecostal church.

In fact, at 14, I worked as a salesgirl at A. Schwab, the second "colored" among a bevy of little old white ladies. We made $3 a day plus commission. There was always a big fight over who would sell the big-ticket items on Saturday. That item was communion sets for churches, and the customers were Black preachers from Tennessee, Arkansas, and Mississippi. The person who made all of those sales was this really fine sister who had worked there forever. But the preachers came in, waiting to see only her!

We went to school by day and usually ended up at the café after school and on the weekends. Mama and Daddy fixed up a room just behind the café where we were expected to do our homework and could sleep if we stayed until closing time. To keep us from being under foot and needing to be entertained, we were often given coins to go to the movies, (2 or 3 a day!), go to the Harlem House to get that hot dog special, go to Pantaze Drug Store on Beale just to look at all the make- up forbidden to us and on Saturday night, sneak onto Beale Street and wait for someone to get thrown out of The King's Palace. The King's Palace had lots of lights and live, loud music, and it had swinging saloon doors that made throwing people out easy.

All of the business owners knew my Daddy's children, kept us safe, and looked after us. We were fearless and quite frankly notoriously curious about any and everything. Beale Street was indeed a street for "colored people." The music always blared on Friday and Saturday night and was all about the Blues. Beale Street represented a culture of 'relief' for her people. Sure, there was sadness, tragedy, fights, and drunk folk. But there was a spirit that said this was 'our' place. Every business owner was 'the law' unto himself because he never wanted White police harassing or abusing his customers. The owners had rules and enforced them to avoid interference from outside the street.

My best memories are of the Cotton Makers Jubilee Carnival in Church Park. When I go to that park now, it seems that surely it was bigger, because the carnival seemed huge to my small life experience. The Cotton Makers Jubilee Parade was simply a thing of pride and dreams. Every little girl wanted to be a majorette, and every boy wanted to be a drummer. We always went early and got a seat in front of Greener's Dry Goods Store (we thought it was a sure enough department store). It was at the corner of Beale, in front of Handy Park, Pantaze Drug Store, and Greener's, that the bands showed their stuff. This also happened during the Christmas parade.

There is so much I could go on about. Why was that Beale Street so different from today's attraction? While there were White and/or Jewish commercial entities on the street, there was a clear spirit of Black ownership from a cultural standpoint. It was our place, our pain, and our pleasure all wrapped up in our food, drink, entertainment, courting, respite from hopelessness, and a prevailing pride of personage.

~ ~ ~ ~ ~

# PREFACE - III

## by
## Dr. Joris Ray

## Former Superintendent, Shelby County (TN) Schools

In reading *"The Metamorphosis of Memphis, the Blues and Beale Street,"* I was fascinated at the segments that chronicle the growth of Memphis. This book is destined to be a classic on Memphis history and its rich culture for the past 200 years. While reading this book, I was overcome with memories of my childhood – hearing stories at the dinner table about where my family came from and tales of how my neighborhood came to be. I may not have understood what it all meant when I was a child, but now, as a leader, I know the groundwork laid down before me and what I must do to continue the mission of those who strived to build a true community.

The author refers to the movers and shakers of Beale Street as "gumbo." That, I had never heard before. When I think of all the ingredients needed to make something so unique, so memorable, and so all-encompassing, it is in fact...gumbo. Each ingredient contributes to the taste without losing its identity. Various cultures and identities brought their know-how, style, and spirit to one pot—Beale Street.

From movies, music, and culture to the fight for civil rights, it is self-evident that Memphis has impacted the world. This book reminds you of the Memphis footprint and opens your eyes to the future of the Bluff City.

Dr. L. LaSimba M. Gray, Jr., walked alongside those fighting for equality and against injustice then and now. His perseverance has never faltered, and like a true educator, he has worked to ensure the youth of tomorrow know our history. In keeping with the use of metaphorical language in music through the ages, he put his words to action, then he "put it on paper."

He is masterful in telling the history of Memphis from a profound perspective. I am proud that he is a product of legacy Memphis City Schools. For all who love Memphis, this book is a must read.

~ ~ ~ ~

The March to Save Black Boys.

Dr. Ray was accompanied by Sheriff Floyd Bonner, County Mayor Lee Harris, Coach Penny Hardaway, Dr. LaSimba Gray, Jr., and Memphis Police Director Rawlings to show collaboration and strength.

# PREFACE - IV

## by
## Menelik Fombi
## Memphis 13

### (1 of the 13 children who integrated the
### Memphis  (TN) City School System in 1961)

In his book, *The Metamorphosis of Memphis, the Blues, and Beale Street,* LaSimba Gray has masterfully connected the dots between significantly epic events in the history of Memphis. This connection that many are aware of  but have failed to recognize is the true evolutionary product of these events.

On a personal note, I have benefited from the passion of LaSimba Gray to preserve this history and to celebrate many of us who helped to make this history. Having been a part of the Civil Rights and Desegregation Movement, I am especially grateful. He has so artfully shared this history in a manner that those of us who helped to make this history feel proud of our accomplishments when we thought we had been so long  forgotten.

Thank you, LaSimba, for this Memphis transformation story and a project worthy of great acclaim!

~ ~ ~ ~ ~

# INTRODUCTION

When I began this project, I had no intentions of writing a book. I began by studying the life and legacy of Robert R. Church, Sr. to advocate his inclusion in the Bicentennial Celebration of Memphis. From the very outset, I became endearingly captivated by the rich history of Memphis, the Blues, and Beale Street. It is without a doubt a genuine understatement to declare that the more I researched, the more I was forced to confront my own formation in the context of Memphis, the Blues, and of Beale Street. I soon developed an insatiable appetite to learn more. Thus began my journey.

I began making frequent visits to the Memphis Public Library, I traveled to pertinent places deemed relevant, I listened anew to blues recordings with a more discriminating purpose, and I positioned myself to talk to musicians and 'Beale Streeters,' who are now few in numbers.

This entire experience has been a true life changer for me. My travels in the Mississippi Delta, meeting people of all ethnic groups, and being able to relate to them out of our mutual love

*Abandoned Juke-Joint in the Mississippi Delta*

for and appreciation of this American music we call the 'Blues' is priceless! Not only did my database grow, but I grew in the acceptance of the universality of humanity. My appreciation grew for the struggle in growing up in a segregated society and benefitting from the sacrifices of courageous individuals of all races. I believe I have become a better person spiritually and emotionally because of what I have learned in this process.

*B. B. King Band*

I must confess, however, as a history buff who loves Memphis, I was limited in my knowledge of the formation and key ingredients that have made Memphis the great city on the 'Fourth' Bluff of the Mississippi River. I have lived in Memphis from the time I was six months old, when my father moved us north to Memphis from Jagoe, Mississippi, in December of 1946. I was in the metamorphosis of Memphis, but so acutely unaware of the movers and shakers who fashioned her culture. In addition, I was also unaware of who gave Memphis her color and who produced her sound. I was unaware of the many unsung heroes and heroines who made indelible contributions, and even those who made the ultimate sacrifice. The personal impact of all of this was, beyond a doubt, absolutely astounding.

In my quest to learn more about the blues, I made frequent trips to the Mississippi Delta. I attended Blues Concerts in the streets, as well as in Juke Joints, and ate fried catfish to the sultry and soulful sounds of Blues Bands. I even visited churches during some of those trips in an effort to affirm the psychological and spiritual connection between Saturday night and Sunday morning. During my travels, I would stop along the way to capture by photograph remnants of an era gone by and to capture quaint sights that still reflected that era. The most impactful experience by far was that of visiting the site, in Money, Mississippi, of the brutal lynching of a young African American boy whose name was Emmett Till. It became blatantly obvious to me that the pain and suffering from that era fueled the emotions expressed in blues lyrics. These internalized music lyrics, which could not be publicly spoken, traveled from the Delta to Memphis in the spirit, mind, and soul of trailblazers such as B.B. King, Bukka T. White, Muddy Waters, Little Milton Campbell, Furry Lewis, T. Bone Walker, and so many others.

I am so indebted to the many strangers who embraced this mission and provided vital information about key personalities, places, and even events involving the formation of Memphis, of the Blues, and of Beale Street. Further included in that vital information was the existence of and contributions of Native Americans, Asian Americans, Italian Americans, Irish Americans, Jewish Americans, and of course African Americans.

In this book, there are names that most Memphians will readily recognize. My research, however, has prompted me to delve in greater

*Black Civil War Soldiers*

detail about the many members of the supporting cast of this development. Few Memphians know the critical significance of the following: the role that Danny Thomas played in preserving Beale Street; the sacrificial role Black Nurses played during the yellow fever epidemic of 1878, which mainly affected White people; Black Soldiers who secured and protected the city during that yellow fever epidemic of 1878, and, that Robert R. Church, Sr. led the efforts to regain the city charter by purchasing the first municipal bond for one thousand dollars.

Yes, we need to know about the contributions from the Roustabouts to the Barons. We need to know the timeline transition of Memphis from a Native American Trading post to a bustling city in the 21st Century. It is this writer's hope and belief that the contributions and sacrifices of historical Memphians will inspire a new generation of "History Makers" as we continue living in and for Memphis, Tennessee.

*Roustabouts*

~ ~ ~ ~ ~

# MY PERSONAL METAMORPHOSIS
# IN MEMPHIS

Jagoe, Mississippi was a small Black Settlement in North Desoto County, Mississippi founded by emancipated Africans following the civil war. Robert Gray, Sr. (author's great grandfather) owned and operated the cotton gin. Haratious Hill, the author's uncle, owned the general store and served as the post-master in the community of Jagoe. The anchoring institution was the New Hope Church founded in 1870 by the Bridgeforth, Saulsbury, Gray, Hill, Baptist, King, Pope, and Abram families. The land was deeded to this group by Thomas O. Bridgeforth. The medical needs of the community were met by Dr. A. J. Jagoe of Hernando, Mississippi. When the post office opened, the settlement was named in honor of Dr. Jagoe.

*The author and twin brother with parents.*

I left Jagoe in 1946 already connected to Beale Street. The Gray family had bonds of friendship with the Schwab family, Beale Street merchants, through years of patronage. In 1923, July 5, James Authur and Maggie Gray welcomed their 12th child into the family. In honor of their friendship, this child was named after Leo Schwab of the Schwab brothers who operated the A. Schwab dry goods store on Beale Street in Memphis. In 1946, Leo and Corrine Gray welcomed twin sons, the first born of the twins was named Leo, Jr. and the second born was named Cleo after Corrine's brother, Cleophus.

After several visits to the A. Schwab store in the Spring of 2019, I was shown a picture of Leo Schwab and the Schwab brothers. Although I legally changed my name in 1995, I still answer to Leo.

The Gray family moved to 373 High Street in 1951, next door to the City Garage. Our 10-member family included my father and mother, Rev. Leo M. Gray, Sr., and Corine Gray; my twin brother, Cleo; and other siblings.

In 1952, I started attending Grant Elementary School at the corner of Auction Avenue and Seventh Street. We walked past the Migliara's Grocery Store on our way to and from school. With our pennies, nickels, and dimes, we would stop at Migliara's Grocery Store at 399 High Street to buy candy and cookies.

One day, I got up enough courage to ask Mr. Lawrence Migliara, the owner, for a job. He asked me what I could do, and I responded, "I can ride a bike, and I want to deliver groceries like Lewis." Lewis Chanault was in his early twenties, and he delivered groceries to all the neighbors on a bicycle. Mr. Lawrence did not think I was old enough, but he told me to come back later.

Then, one day, out of the clear blue sky, Mr. Lawrence asked me if I wanted to throw circulars. I was hired on, and Lawrence, Jr., would take us to various sections of the community and drop us off on one end of a street and pick us up at the other end. Circulars were thrown on Thursdays of each week, advertising the sales for the weekend at the store. I made a whopping 75 cents. But that job led to my sweeping the store, inside and out front, and emptying trash. I was made to feel a part of the Migliara family. When they ate lunch, I ate. When "little" Lawrence got candy, I got candy.

When we heard about Scola Brothers' Super Market at 653 North Parkway paying $3.00 for two days' work, a group of us went over to apply. Mr. Tony, one of the brothers, would come to the parking lot and screen us by testing us to repeat the sales pitch for the week: "Scola Brothers got eggs 29 cents a dozen, lard 15 cents a pound, neck bones 13 cents a pound, and plenty fresh vegetables." I was hired and worked at that job for two years.

An elderly neighbor, Mr. Jones, asked my parents if I could work a few nights with him to clean some hardwood floors at the Weild Brothers Cotton Company at 93 South Front Street. Mr. Jones had gotten too old to get down on his knees and scrub floors. When I was ten years old, my parents granted me permission when Mr. Jones assured them that I would be home before 10:00 pm and that he would feed me. My job was to take steel wool and scrub the corners and along the baseboards of the offices to remove built up wax. I worked on that job until my fingers were too sore to touch. Because of my sore fingers, I began to avoid Mr. Jones and would leave home about the time he would come to pick me up. When my dad questioned me about missing my pickup, I showed him my fingers, and he said, "Tell Mr. Jones you cannot continue, so he won't be counting on you."

At the age of eleven, I was old enough to go to the fields in Arkansas to pick cotton. I was excited until I learned that you were paid by the pounds you picked. There were people who could pick two or three hundred pounds per day. I would pick next to my mother, who would pick 170 pounds a day, and I could barely pick 75 pounds. I don't think I was ever more frustrated in my young life.

Racial tension in the neighborhood escalated when Hurt Village was constructed adjacent to the campus of Grant School. The School Board built a seven-foot brick wall to divide our campus from the property of Hurt Village. Hurt Village was a Memphis housing project built for Whites. There was a gang in the 'Village' that did not want Blacks to walk through the Village. Whenever Blacks walked through the Village, the alarm cry was, *"N----er in the Village!"* We knew then we had been spotted, and, for our safety, we had to outrun the members of their gang.

Then one afternoon, a White boy, David Denton, was drowning in the bayou that ran between Second Street and Mill Avenue. David Norris, a seventh grader at Grant School, dove into the bayou and saved the boy's life. The next morning, during devotion, the principal, Mr. Robert Morris, saluted David over the intercom for his heroic act of risking his life to save the White boy, and there was a spontaneous applause throughout the school. At lunchtime, everybody wanted to see David Norris. He was the first hero I saw rise from the ranks of a schoolmate.

I remember vividly how David struggled to dress for school. His shoes were ragged and run over. His pants were dingy and wrinkled. But, before the week ended, White men made several trips to Grant School to bring David gifts of clothing and a brand new red and white bicycle. David had new Levi jeans and penny loafers. He was a city-wide hero and helped to ease the tensions between Grant School students and the residents of Hurt Village. A local songwriter wrote the following song about Davis Norris and recorded it to the tune of David Crockett.

> *While walking by the bayou one evening after school*
> *He hadn't learned his lesson nor the Golden Rule*
> *All of a sudden, he heard a boy yell*
> *He jumped in the water swimming fast and  swell*
> *David, David Norris, King  of the old Grant School.*

Then, in the late 50's, the announcement came, we had to move. The Interstate 40 was coming through our neighborhood. We were excited about the new house in the Alcy-Ball community. It had a large backyard with pear and peach trees. We even had a large grape vine running along the fence. The Bellevue Drive-In movie screen could be seen from our front yard. But all of that excitement diminished drastically when grief set in from losing classmates and teachers I had been with since first grade and now having to leave good old Grant School.

When I made some adjustments, I was ready to find some work after school and on weekends. There was a Vanucci Big Star grocery store on Bellevue next to the Bellevue Drive-In movie theatre. I was hired and worked sacking groceries, cleaning floors, restrooms, and the parking lot. The fun was receiving tips for sacking and taking groceries to the cars of customers. Mr. Vernon Presley was the customer every sacker wanted to serve. The father of Elvis Presley was a big tipper and whoever sacked his groceries had bragging rights for a week.

On the west side of Bellevue, in the same block, was the Vanucci Italian Restaurant. I was hired there and learned to cook under the tutelage of Mr. Toby Hullum, the head chef. I kept that job until I made the football team at Hamilton High School in 1962. But, because of the practice schedule and games, I had to resign. Mrs. Beretta had a restaurant on Airways Boulevard and invited me to work for her on weekends. I never saw Mrs. Beretta dress casually. She was always dressed immaculately in high heels, and her face was always made up as if she were taking a photograph or posing for a fashion magazine. I gladly accepted the position of janitor and kept it until I graduated in the Spring of 1964. I was then ready for the big time and accepted a job at the Shainberg's Black and White Department Store on Main Street, one block north of Beale Street, where I made $1.25 per hour and could go moseying down Beale Street after work. My objective for working was to save money and go off to college in the Fall of 1964.

I mention my employment history here because of my exposure to diversity in culture. I worked for Southern White plantation owners in Arkansas and Italian and Jewish business owners and Black entrepreneurs in Memphis. I learned many lessons in life working around and for different ethnic groups. The main lessons I learned were the power of family unity and the improved self-esteem garnered from economic independence. At the age of ten, I started to help my dad by buying my own clothes and paying my own school fees. I shopped at the Dollar General Stores, Goodwill Stores, Shainberg's Black and White Department Store, and shops on Beale Street. I learned to find bargains and use the "Lay Away System" early in my life. The "Lay Away System" taught me that delayed gratification was worth waiting for, as long as you were honest and willing to work.

~ ~ ~ ~ ~

# ACKNOWLEDGEMENTS

I am tremendously indebted to my many friends and colleagues who have endured my constant string of questions about Memphis, the blues and Beale Street. I am thankful to my daughter, Angelique Gray, for her graphic skills and professional advice to make this book appealing, interesting, inspirational and, most of all, informative. I am thankful to my daughter, Dr. Leah Monette Gray, for making sure my glasses properly fit and that the bi-focal and transitional lenses served me well.

The staff of the Benjamin Hooks Library, and especially Sir Wayne Dowdy, have been indispensable. This staff made research enjoyable. Judy Piser always had information I could readily use at the Southern Folklore Center. I am indebted to the strangers who volunteered information, made referrals and encouraged me during my three trips to the Delta. The Shelby County Archives, directed by Frank Stewart, provided photographs I had not seen since 1959—The Migliara's Grocery Store, at High Street and Concord Avenue, where I worked and the City Garage that housed the Cotton Carnival Celebrity Horses of cowboys Gene Autry, Pancho and the Cisco Kidd, Wild Bill, Jingles, and Roy Rogers and Dale Evans. These television stars had to pass our house twice daily during the Annual Cotton Carnival in Memphis. Seeing photographs of a beloved community that was demolished to make way for the Interstate-40 Expressway brought back many fond memories. Thanks, Frank.

My heartfelt thanks to the readers of my manuscript: Rev. John Glaze, Markum L. Stansbury, Carol Gray, my special advisor and proofreader, Dr. George Grant (my original publisher), and Myles Wilson, who freely gave information on the "Chitlin Circuit" and "Juke Joints" of West Tennessee. To the New Hope Baptist Church of Jago, Mississippi (now Southaven, Mississippi); the St. Mark Baptist Church of Wilkinsville, Tennessee; and the historic New Sardis Baptist Church, in Germantown,

Tennessee — I am grateful for the financial insulation provided to allow me to participate in prophetic ministry for 50 years. Thanks also to Dr. Sherman Helton, Rev. E. Allen Redwell, and my beloved son in the ministry, Rev. Darrell Harrington.

I owe special thanks to Rev. Dwight 'Gatemouth' Moore for befriending me and pouring out his experiences on Beale Street into my spirit; my spiritual mentor, the late Dr. Benjamin L. Hooks, who demonstrated prophetic ministry with priestly devotion for more than 50 years; and Rev. Samuel B. Kyles for sharing the leadership of Operation PUSH.

If this project is of any literary value, it is so because readers remain willing to share the metamorphosis of Memphis, the Blues and Beale Street with the author, who continues to be a work in progress. I sincerely hope that all readers will be inspired to do greater research into the rich history of Memphis. Once you learn Memphis history, resolve to make history in Memphis.

L. LaSimba M. Gray, Jr.<br>Memphis, Tennessee

# METAMORPHOSIS OF MEMPHIS
# ON THE MISSISSIPPI RIVER

In 1818, the land on the Fourth Bluff on the Mississippi River still belonged to the Chickasaw Nation of Native Americans. In the Treaty of Tuscaloosa (also known as Jackson Purchase), signed in October 11 and ratified in 1819 by the United States Congress, the Chickasaw Nation ceded their land to the United States. Shortly thereafter, the city of Memphis was founded by Andrew Jackson, James Winchester, and John Overton.

This unusual name in developing America may have been a marketing strategy—or simply James Winchester's fascination with Egyptian antiquity. His fascination could have been the result of the French invasion of Egypt in 1798. At the end of the War of 1812, America was seized by the rekindled interest in classical history and the marvels of Egypt. A Memphis on the fourth bluff in Tennessee on the mighty Mississippi River would prick the curiosity of the public.

James Winchester was known for his passion for classical history and his tremendous admiration of Egyptian influence on the world. His passion had been demonstrated in Middle Tennessee when he named a small town, Cairo, in 1798. It has been suggested that Winchester had hopes of Cairo being named the capitol of Tennessee. That hope was dashed when Nashville was named the capitol in 1843. Cairo, Tennessee faded into oblivion and became a ghost town in the shadow of Nashville.

Winchester's passion for classical history was further demonstrated in the naming of the Winchester children — Brutus, Marcus, Selina, Lucillius, Alimira, Napoleon, Valerius, and Publicola. The naming of children, places and events reflects the thinking of those assigning the names.

The name Memphis was appropriate because of the similarities between Memphis on the Nile River and the geographical setting of the land on the fourth bluff on the Mississippi. Both cities were positioned at the apex of a fertile delta. Memphis on the Nile River was a major distribution center and Memphis on the Mississippi River had the potential to duplicate that same function. Memphis on the Nile was a bustling hub of commerce, political impact and cultural development. Memphis on the Mississippi had the same potential and realized that potential in the mid-1800's. The Nile River is 4,130 miles long and touches eleven countries in its northern flow. The Mississippi River is 2,348 miles long and touches ten states in its southern flow to the Gulf of Mexico. Memphis on the Nile was the capital city of Egypt during the reign of Pharaoh Menes. Memphis on the Mississippi is often referred to as the capital of Mississippi because of the cotton industry.

The name, Memphis, means "Established and Beautiful." On a personal note, I grew up in Memphis when Memphis was known as "City Beautiful." Every spring, there was a "Clean Up, Fix Up, Paint Up" city-wide campaign. All streets were swept clean overnight. Memphis was once known as the "Cleanest and Quietest" city in America. I now know the connection.

African American scholar, Mo Lefi K. Asante would have declared that James Winchester was using "Afrocentric thinking" when he named the fourth bluff on the Mississippi River, Memphis. Afrocentric thinking is processing events through an African world view. The Rev. Dr. William "Bill" Adkins may have to take second place to James Winchester in using Afrocentric thinking in Memphis, Tennessee, or remain the first in modern times to use Afrocentric thinking in Memphis.

Memphis developed into a world market for cotton during the early years of the 19th century. Cotton was king and slaves were needed to break the ground, plant the seeds, cultivate, and harvest the white gold of the South. Therefore, Memphis became the largest slave-trading city in the South. Located on the fourth bluff was key to this dubious distinction. Memphis is mid-way between Natchez, Mississippi and St. Louis, Missouri. Memphis sits at the apex of the Delta. The economic engine of the Delta is cotton, without rival.

Memphis was also convenient for plantation owners from Arkansas, Southeastern Missouri, West Tennessee, Northern Mississippi, and

Northeast Louisiana to trade cotton and secure labor (slaves). In 1857, there were twelve slave traders advertising in the local media. Circulars were nailed on posts and on walls throughout the downtown Memphis area. Advertisements graded the enslaved as one would market cattle, horses, or mules.

Because of the slave trade and the growing economy, the demand for labor was on the increase in Memphis and Shelby County. Correspondingly, the black population grew.

In the mid-1800's, Memphis became the largest exporter of cotton in the world. The growth was explosive. In 1836, 10,000 bales of cotton were shipped from Memphis to the world market. In 1849, 140,000 bales of cotton were shipped from Memphis. In 1852, Memphis rose to become the second largest river port on the Mississippi River. Cotton was king, and Memphis was enjoying the building boom, population growth, the construction of a railroad system, the United States Navy Yard, and the emerging steamboat industry.

This phenomenal growth had a corresponding demand for labor. That labor would come from the trans-Atlantic slave trade. Initially, the slave trade was conducted in private transactions. When the competition increased, slave markets were introduced. The competition for sales led to open markets and advertising in the local printed media. Advertisements to buy and sell slaves were as common as advertisements to buy and sell mules, wagons, and dry goods.

Leaders of this despicable practice were Ike Bolton, Tom Dickens, Byrd Hillard and Nathan B. Forrest. These men formed corporations and entered into fierce competition that down spiraled into bloody, deadly family feuds.

The public display of slaves for sale was another step in the indignation and dehumanization process of enslaved Africans. On the auction blocks, their personhood was stripped away and humanity demeaned. The enslaved were considered property.

The legendary poet and folk singer, Oscar Brown, Jr., offers a riveting perspective on slave auctions in his, "Bid 'Em In,"

## Bid 'em in! Bid 'em in!

Now that sun is hot and plenty bright
Let's get down to business and get home tonight
Bid 'em in!
Auctioning slaves is a real high art
Bring that young gal, Roy, She's good for a start
*Bid 'em in! Get 'em in!*

Now, here's a real good buy, only about fifteen
Her great grand mammy was a Dahomey queen.
Just look at her face, she sure ain't homely
Like Sheba in the Bible, she's black but comely
*Bid 'em in!*

Gonna start her at three. Can I hear three?
Step up gents.  Take a good look and see
Cause I know you'll want her once you've seen her
She's young and ripe. Make a darn good breeder
*Bid 'em in!*

She's good in the fields.  She can sew and cook
Strip her down, Roy, let the gentlemen look
She's full up front and ample behind
Examine her teeth, if you got a mind
*Bid 'em in!*

Here's a bid of three from a man who is thrifty
Three twenty five! Can I hear three fifty?
Your money ain't earning you much in the bank
Turn her around, Roy, let 'em look at her flanks
*Bid 'em in!*

Three fifty's the bid.  I am looking for four
At four hundred dollars, she's a bargain sho

Four is the bid. Four fifty.  Five?
Five hundred dollars. Now, look alive
*Bid 'em in!*

Don't mind her tears.  That's one of her tricks
Five fifty's bid and who'll say six?
She's healthy and strong and well equipped
Make a fine lady's maid when she's properly whipped
*Bid 'em in! Get 'em in!*

Six! Six fifty! Don't be slow
Seven is the bid. Gonna let her go.
At seven, she's going!
Going!
Gone!

Pull her down, Roy, Bring the next one on
*Bid 'em in! Get 'em in! Bid 'em in!*

This hopeless status of being a slave was depressing, demeaning, and disgusting. The Africans were enslaved and helpless. It was a daily mental struggle to survive.

In the early 1850's, Memphis had relaxed rules to govern the slave population in comparison to other regions of the South. The enslaved were allowed to hire out their time to other employers, in addition to their masters.  Slaves had some latitude in determining where they lived and for whom they worked.  This relaxed control of slaves lasted until citizens petitioned the City Council in 1855.

The petition called for more control of slave labor and made it unlawful to hire a slave without the permission of the slave's owner; prohibited slaves from living with other ethnic groups and required slaves to have in their possession written permits for them to be on the streets after dark. The challenges of controlling slaves brought on unique problems labeled "Urban slavery."  On the plantations of the rural, slaves worked from sunup to sundown. There was very little time for a social life on the plantation, but in the city, there was simply not enough work to occupy all of the time of a slave.

Major problems of Urban Slavery:
1. Where would the slaves live in a segregated society?
2. Who would supervise the slaves when they hired out their time?
3. The question of loyalty was a constant concern.
4. To what extent did the practice of slaves hiring out their time weaken the institution of slavery?
5. The high percentage of slaves in the general population.

A campaign was launched to distribute slave labor to plantations. It was thought that slave labor was too expensive to be wasted on urban life. In the rural, slave labor demands were on the rise.

While Memphis enjoyed the economic engine found in slavery, the abolitionary movement was growing in other segments of the country. The matter of slavery was the breaking point for these United States of America. When Frances Wright arrived in America in 1825, she became an advocate for emancipation of the enslaved Africans. Her solution to the problem was to train the enslaved in agricultural skills and allow plantation owners to draw from the trained pool of Africans to operate their plantations. The twist so unusual in Wright's approach was the Africans would become free men and women and would be free to work for whomever they chose. This concept was not well received by the plantation owners nor the beneficiaries of the cotton industry and agricultural enterprises of the South.

To demonstrate her concept, Frances Wright created an idealistic community called the "Neshoba Experiment" in 1826 in the Germantown area on 320 acres. She then went to the slave auction and purchased 30 slaves to live in the Neshoba Community. These slaves were purchased to be emancipated through training and the ability to purchase their freedom. In Frances Wright's mind, this would be a win-win situation for the enslaved and society in general.

Frances Wright wanted to end slavery on the premise of the declaration of Independence that, "We hold these truths to be self-evident, that all men are created equal, that they are endowed by their creator with certain unalienable rights." In fact, it was the United States Declaration of Independence that attracted Frances Wright to America.

*Frances Wright*

When she purchased the 320 acres of land (later expanded to 2,000 acres), she physically joined the efforts to clear the land and built cabins. She participated in the farming chores and led the recruitment of residents to live in Neshoba. The land was located in a mosquito-infested area and Frances contracted malaria and had to leave the community to recover. During her absence, appointed managers instituted programs and policies that contradicted the founding principles of Neshoba. Punishment for slaves became frequent and inhumane.

James Richardson, a White supervisor, openly involved himself sexually with a Black woman named Josephine Lalotte. Their relationship led to negative publicity on interracial relationships and free sexual relationships in the community. These reports led to the increased opposition of the experiment and demands to close it down. When the Neshoba Experiment ended in 1830, Frances Wright chartered a ship and transported the 30 slaves to Haiti to live as free men and women.

Frances Wright may have failed at her Neshoba Experiment, but she earned, without trying, a seat at the Table-of-Nobility for decency and human rights. One cannot arrange a meeting with Ida B. Wells- Barnett, William Lloyd Garrison, President Abraham Lincoln, Frederick Douglas, Robert G. Shaw, Horace Greely, Charlotte F. Grimkle, Rev. John Brown, Rev. Nat Turner, Rev. Harriet Tubman, Sojourner Truth, Wendell Phillips, William Wilberforce, and the Quaker Community without a reserved seat for Frances Wright.

Following the Civil War, the concerns shifted from too much labor to "Will we have enough labor?" In 1869, the Chamber of Commerce of Memphis sponsored a conference to address the anticipated shortage of labor in the post-emancipation era. The objective of the conference was to develop strategies to recruit Asians to migrate to Memphis. Five hundred interested citizens attended the conference.

It is literally impossible to cover, in one volume, adequate details of the extensive history of Memphis for the past 200 years. However, I trust that the following timeline will give Memphians an appetite for more research and a deeper appreciation for the contributions made by Native Americans, Enslaved Africans, and all immigrants who came to the Memphis area at the beginning of the 19th century.

~ ~ ~ ~ ~

# Memphis Blues and Beale Street Timeline

**1818** **(1819) Land** was purchased from the Chickasaw Nation by the U.S. government in 1818 for $300,000, to be paid in $15,000 annual installments over 20 years. On May 22, 1819, Memphis was founded by John Overton, James Winchester, and Andrew Jackson, who bought the John Rice Grant (5,000 acres) for $2,500. The new city was named after the ancient capital of Egypt on the Nile River.

**1819 - Surveyor, William Lawrence** laid out the blueprint of the **City of Memphis** and the proprietors divided the first lots (April-May). Inhabitants petitioned the Tennessee legislature for the establishment of a county. The petition was approved in November and Shelby County was established and named in honor of Kentucky Governor Isaac Shelby, a Revolutionary War hero and the first governor of Kentucky.

**1820 - Postal service** began and the State of Tennessee opened a Land office in Memphis.

**1824 (1825) - The Sanderlin's Bluff,** north of Memphis, was selected to be the county seat of Shelby County. It was later renamed Raleigh in 1825 by Joseph Graham to reflect his North Carolina roots.

**1825 - Frances Wrigh**t, a Scottish-born abolitionist, arrived near Memphis and founded the Nashoba community (on about 320 acres along the Wolf River, ~13 miles east of the city) to pilot a model of self-emancipation for enslaved individuals. She was the first American woman to speak publicly against slavery.

**1826 - Frances Wright** established the "Nashoba Experiment" near Germantown, Tennessee, aiming to promote the self-emancipation of enslaved individuals. With the tacit support of James Winchester, Wright purchased enslaved people with the intention of training them in self-sufficiency and eventually granting them their freedom.

**1826 - Marcus Winchester** was elected the first mayor of Memphis. Winchester was the son of one of Memphis's founders, James Winchester, and played a significant role in the city's early development.

**1828 - First Yellow Fever Epidemic** in Memphis 650 cases, 150 deaths.

**1830 - The Indian Removal Act,** signed by President Andrew Jackson, authorized the federal government to negotiate treaties exchanging Native American lands in the East for territory west of the Mississippi River.

**1830 - A Town Hall** was built in Memphis, with a population of 662.

**1833-** **The Farmers and Merchants Bank,** the first bank in Memphis, Tennessee was established by Ike Rawlings.

**1835** **LaGrange and Memphis Railroad** was organized.

**1839 -** **Robert R. Church, Sr.** was born in Holly Springs, Mississippi.

**1842 -** The first major hotel in Memphis, **The Gayoso House**, was built by Robertson Topp.

**1846 -** **South Memphis** was incorporated by Robertson Topp.

**1849 -** **Memphis and South Memphis** were merged into one united city.

**1850 -** **The Population** of Memphis reached 8,841.

**1851 -** **Robert Church, Sr.** arrived in Memphis to live with his father and became his father's understudy in bookkeeping, cabin boy and steward.

**1852 -** **Memphis Riverport,** on the Mississippi River, emerged as the third largest port to only the St. Louis and the New Orleans Ports.

**1857 -** **The Memphis Charleston Railroad** was completed linking Memphis to the Atlantic Coast.

**1861 -** 3,000 Citizens voted unanimously for **secession.** The Confederate Army headquarters and supply depot were set up in Memphis.

**1862 -** **Ida B. Wells** was born into slavery in Holly Springs, Mississippi. She never ceased her struggle for dignity and freedom.

**1862 -** **Union Forces** defeated the Confederacy in Memphis and established a headquarters, supply depot and hospital. Steamer, Victoria, was captured by the Federal Fleet during the "Battle of Memphis." This allowed Robert R. Church, Sr., to set up for business in Memphis.

**1862 -** **A prisoner of war camp** was established along with a refugee camp for slaves in Memphis by the Union Army. General Ulysses S. Grant set up his headquarters in Memphis on Beale Street in the Hunt-Phelan Mansion.

**1862 -** **Fort Pickering** was established on the South Bluff by the Union Army when Memphis surrendered during the Civil War. Today, Fort Pickering is the site of the French Fort Neighborhood, Chickasaw Heritage Park, the Navy Hospital and the Metal Museum. The former Navy Hospital is now being renovated to house luxury apartments.

**1863** - The former **City Hospital** was relocated to the Botanical Medical College on Beale Street in preparation for injuries and casualties of the Civil War. This was a part of the move to secure 5,000 hospital beds for Grant's Campaign in Vicksburg, Mississippi.

**1864** - **Martial law** was proclaimed in Memphis.

**1864** - **The First National Bank of Memphis** received Charter #336 under the new National Bank Act of the Lincoln Administration. Today, the First National Bank of Memphis, now the First Horizon Bank, is the 14th oldest bank in the United States.

**1865** - **The Civil War** ended and Reconstruction began.

**1865** - **The Freedman's Bureau** was set up in Memphis.

**1866** - **Race riots,** conducted by Irish policemen, led to the random killing of 48 African Americans, injuring hundreds, burning schools for African Americans and businesses owned by African Americans. This scandal was investigated by the Freedman's Bureau. Robert R. Church, Sr., while protecting his property, was shot and left for dead, but he lived to testify before federal investigators. This became a national scandal.

**1869** - **The Memphis Chamber of Commerce** held a conference to recruit Chinese laborers to fill the void expected by the emancipation of African laborers. The attendance at the conference was estimated to be over 500 people.

**1870** - **LeMoyne College** was founded on Beale and Orleans streets by the American Missionary Association.

**1871** - **Christian Brothers College** was organized as a private Catholic institution of higher learning in Memphis. It merged with Siena College in 1970, becoming co-educational. In 1990, University status was granted to Christian Brothers, the oldest collegiate degree granting institution in Memphis.

**1873** - **William Christopher Handy** was born in Florence, Alabama.

**1874** - **Edward Hull Crump** was born October 2, 1874, in Holly Springs, Mississippi. (Robert R. Church, Sr. and Edward Crump were both born in Holly Springs, Mississippi.)

**1875 - Robert R. Church Jr.** was born in the family home at 384 S. Lauderdale in Memphis, Tennessee.

**1876 - A. Schwab** opened on Beale Street to sell dry goods and family supplies to African Americans of the Greater Mid-South. The main attraction was numerous sales and hospitality not found on Main Street.

*Schwab Brothers*

**1878 - The Fifth Yellow Fever Epidemic** hit Memphis in late July, causing 5,150 deaths of the more than 17,600 cases. Shortly after the plague was officially announced, 25,000 citizens left Memphis, reducing the city's population to 19,000, of which 14,000 were Blacks. However, Blacks remained and took care of the sick, buried the dead, protected property and patrolled the streets of Memphis.

**1879 - The State of Tennessee** declared Memphis bankrupt and repealed the city charter.

**1879 - The Sixth Yellow Fever Epidemic** hit Memphis; real estate value drastically dropped and Robert R. Church, Sr., expanded his real estate holdings in Memphis.

**1882 - Lymus Wallace** was elected to a four-year term as alderman, becoming the first African American to serve in Memphis Government.

**1884 - Ida B. Wells** was a teacher at the legendary Woodstock School in Woodstock, Tennessee and rode the Chesapeake/Ohio Railroad to Woodstock daily. When forced to sit in the section with laborers and in direct line of smoke and soot, she filed a lawsuit in the Circuit Court against the Chesapeake and Ohio Railroad for not making first class seating available to Blacks. She won the lawsuit and was awarded $500 for damages.

*Ida B. Wells Historic Marker*

**1885 - George Battier**, the White owner of the Battier Drug store  on Beale Street, was indicted on miscegenation charge for marrying a Black woman  by the name Mary Burton.  Although the couple lived openly as man and wife, charges were brought to enforce the separation of the races in Memphis.  The court exonerated them on July 27, 1885.

**1886 - Cash Mosby**, a Negro entrepreneur, organized train excursions and tours for rural Blacks to visit Beale Street. Many excursionists became residents of Beale Street.

**1888 - Howe Institute** was founded on Beale Street with the generosity of Jerome Howe, a White benefactor from Illinois. Its main focus was to  train clergy for the ministry.  The legendary Rev. C. L. Franklin and Bishop J. O. Patterson, Sr. were outstanding students at the Howe Institute.

*Bishop J. O. Patterson*

**1890- Ida B. Wells** began publishing the *Memphis Free Speech Newspaper* on Beale Street.  This was the beginning of 'advocacy journalism.'  Her mission was to end lynching and gain civil rights for African Americans.

*Robert R. Church, Sr.*

**1890 - Robert R. Church, Sr.** purchased the first municipal bond to pay off the city's debt. His act of courage and faith in Memphis led other citizens to purchase $200,000 in municipal bonds.

**1890 – Elzey Eugene Meacham**, a white real estate developer, purchased land from the Deaderick family, whose 5,000-acre plantation was originally established by John George Deaderick in the early 1800s. Meachem developed part of that land into **Orange Mound**, one of the first subdivisions in the United States specifically designed to provide African Americans with the opportunity for homeownership. The neighborhood was historically bounded by the Southern Railroad to the north, Airways Boulevard to the west, Park Avenue to the south, and Goodwyn Street to the east.

**1893 - The State of Tennessee** restored the charter of the City of Memphis.

**1897 - Bishop Charles Harrison Mason** founded the Church of God in Christ in Memphis, Tennessee.  The Church today has between 6 - 8 million

Church Park Auditorium

members worldwide.

**1899 - Robert R. Church, Sr**. built the Church Park Auditorium on Beale Street for African Americans without a dime of taxpayer's money. He built the facility after the City of Memphis failed to build parks for African Americans.

**1901 - The New Chicago Community** was founded in the North Memphis area to meet the housing needs of a growing industrial complex anchored by the Firestone Tire and Rubber Company. The late Matthew W. Davis, Sr. served as its honorary mayor for many years.

W. C. Handy

**1905 - W. C. Handy** moved to Memphis at the invitation of Matthew Thornton to train and conduct his band, The Knights of Pythians. Handy became contaminated by the "Beale Street itch" and wrote, "I'd rather be there than any place I know."

**1905 - Dr. W. E. B. Dubois**, a noted scholar, collaborated with Harry Pace to publish the Moon Magazine on Beale Street.

W. E. B. DuBois

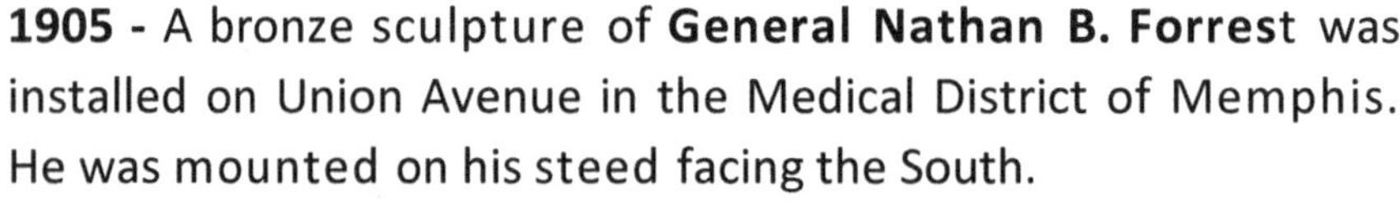

**1905 -** A bronze sculpture of **General Nathan B. Forrest** was installed on Union Avenue in the Medical District of Memphis. He was mounted on his steed facing the South.

Hooks Brothers Marker

**1906 - Robert R. Church, Sr.** gave leadership to the establishment of Solvent Savings Bank and Trust on Beale Street.

**1906 – The Memphis Zoo** was established in Overton Park following a proposal by Colonel Robert Galloway, a park commissioner and newspaper editor. Supported by the Memphis Park Commission, the zoo began with modest enclosures and quickly grew with community backing. It would later receive organizational support from the Memphis Zoological Society, incorporated in 1910.

**1907 - Hooks Brothers Photographers** operated a viable business at 164 Beale Street. Their specialty was to remove blemishes off the skin. Acne and scars never showed up in photos taken by the Hooks Brothers. Robert and Henry Hooks owned and operated the studio at 164 Beale Street.

**1907 - The University of West Tennessee College of Medicine and Surgery** relocated to Memphis from Jackson, Tennessee. Dr. Miles V. Lynk was founder and President. The college also offered degrees in dentistry, pharmacy, nursing and law. Its mission was to train Black professionals when other institutions denied them enrollment.

**1909 - W.C. Handy** composed a campaign tune reportedly used during Edward H. Crump's mayoral campaign in Memphis. Handy later developed and published the piece in 1912 under the title "The Memphis Blues," which became one of the earliest published blues compositions.

**1910 - The Fraternal Savings Bank** was organized by J. Jay Scott and H. Wayman Wilkerson. The Fraternal and Solvent Savings Bank and the Trust Bank later merged.

**1910 - Collins Chapel Hospital** was founded by the Christian Methodist Episcopal Church after Mrs. Lillie McNeil donated her two- story home to the church. In 1938, its name was changed to The Collins Chapel Connectional Hospital, Inc. Dr. William Martin and John T. Wilson provided medical services and directions for the budding institution. It was the only hospital locally where African Americans could receive medical treatment until segregation ended.

*Collins Chapel Hospital*

**1912 - August 29, Robert R. Church, Sr.** succumbed to heart disease. His death was considered a major victory in that he died of natural causes. Robert Church, Sr., had survived slavery, the Civil War and numerous attempts on his life. Robert R. Church, Jr. then stepped from the shadow of his father well prepared to lead the Black community in politics, business and philanthropy.

**1912 - W.C. Handy** published the **Memphis Blues.**

**1912** - **The University of Memphis** was established in Memphis as the West Tennessee State Normal School.

**1916** - **Robert R. Church, Jr.** organized and funded the **Lincoln League** expressly to register African Americans to vote. Memphis was the only southern city that did not disenfranchise the African American citizens following the Reconstruction era.

**1917** - **W.C. Handy** published the national hit **"Beale Street Blues"** and the national musical spotlight turned to Memphis.

*The Beale Street Blues*

**1917** - **Robert R. Church, Jr.** organized the **Memphis Branch of the National Association for the Advancement of Colored People (NAACP)**, the very first branch in Tennessee.

**1920** - **Abe Plough** expanded Plough Chemical Company's operations to Beale Street in Memphis, growing the business he originally founded in 1908 at age 16 into a leading producer of pharmaceutical and consumer products.

*Joseph E. Walker*

**1923** - **Universal Life Insurance Company** was founded **by Dr. Joseph E. Walker.**

**1923** - **The Chickasaw Gardens Community** was developed at the former home site of Clarence Saunders, founder of the Piggly Wiggly Grocery Store chain. Mr. Saunders lost the property during the Great Depression. Developers then developed his property into one of the most affluent neighborhoods in the nation, punctuated with some of the finest real estate in Memphis.

**1923** - **The Memphis Red Sox** joined the National Negro Baseball League. The team was later purchased by the Martin Brothers, J. B. Martin and Dr. B. B. Martin, and played at Martin Stadium at Crump Blvd and Lauderdale Street in South Memphis. One of the players on the Red Socks team was the legendary country singer, Charley Pride.

**1923** - **Samuel Cornelius Phillips**, aka Sam Phillips, was born in Florence, Alabama. He became known as the "Father of Rock & Roll" music. He was one of the greatest of the Rock & Roll music genre. (Note: He and W. C. Handy were both born in Florence.)

**1923** -  Former Memphis **Mayor Henry Loeb** was born on December 9, 1923, and died on September 8, 1992. He served as mayor of Memphis for two different terms, 1960-1963 and 1968-1971, and is known for his resistance to the demands of the Sanitation Workers for improved working conditions in 1968.

**1925** - **Southwestern College**, later named Rhodes College, relocated to Memphis to occupy a 123-acre wooded site adjacent to the Historic Hein Park Community in Mid-Town.

**1926** -  **Dr. Joseph Edison Walker** organized the **Negro Chamber of Commerce** in Memphis.

**1926** - **Jimmy Lunceford,** from Fulton Mississippi, arrived on Beale Street and impacted the "Beale Street Sound' and the nation with mostly high school students from Manassas High School. The group was named the "Chickasaw Syncopators." Manassas High School would later produce musical giants, such as Hank Crawford, Evelyn Young, Isaac Hayes, Ford Nelson, Sidney Kirk, Onzie Horn and William Hurd.

*Jimmy Lunceford*

**1927** - *The Memphis Press Scimitar* reported the discovery of a *Black Book* by the Deputy Prohibition Officer, A.J. Howe. The *Black Book* was owned by Jon Belomini, a bootlegger on Beale Street. Belomini, kept meticulous records of bribes and pay offs to Memphis police detectives and deputy sheriffs. The payments were made to some 38 officers to look the other way to protect Belomini's empire.

**1927** - **Richard Wright**, author and Lecturer, left Memphis for Chicago for better career opportunities. He became a literary giant after marinating on Beale Street for two years. He later authored *Native Son*, a celebrated novel. Wright attended the Howe Institute in Memphis during his early years.

*Richard Wright*

**1927** - **Victor Recording Company** began recording sessions in Memphis. Their primary focus was the musical sounds of Beale Street.

**1929** - **Memphis Technical High School** opened to meet the skills needed in local industries.  It was established in the Anti-bellum mansion of P. Van Vleet, a successful wholesale druggist.

**1933 - Beale Street** was shut down by the Memphis Police to rid the city of vice and bootlegging. Beale Street became as dry as a desert and the graveyard for bootleggers. *"Take me to the River"* had new meaning in 1933, according to W. C. Handy.

**1933 - Machine Gun Kelly** was captured while staying at a friend's home at 1408 Rayner in South Memphis near Hamilton High School.

**1942 - Aretha Franklin** was born in Memphis to the family of Rev. C. L. Franklin.

*B.B. King*

**1946 - B. B. King** left the Mississippi Delta, headed for Memphis to pursue his dreams. He found those dreams on Beale Street. (See, "Beale Street Gumbo")

**1948 The Radio Station, WDIA,** changed its programing from "country" to an all African American programming by owner, Bert Ferguson. Nat D. Williams was hired as its first Black Disc Jockey.

*Bert Ferguson*

**1949 - WHBQ,** a radio station formatted for country music, started to play Black music. Dewey Phillips led the charge with his "Red, Hot and Blue" radio show. (See, "Beale Street Gumbo")

**1950 - Sam Phillips** opened a recording studio in Memphis to make records with local talent. The mission was inclusive of Black artists. This venture in the recording industry was the genesis of capturing the Memphis sound.

**1952 - Owen Junior College,** named to honor Dr. Samuel Owen, a local pastor and state and national Baptist leader, was founded in Memphis, Tennessee.

**1955- Danny Thomas** organized the **St. Jude Children's Research Hospital** in Memphis. (See, "Danny Thomas and Beale Street")

**1957 - The WDIA Goodwill Revue** featured Elvis Presley and B.B. King. Both had been participants at Amateur Nights on Beale Street.

**1957 - Stax Records** was founded as Satellite Records in South Memphis. In 1961, the label became Stax Records, recognizing the founders, Jim Stewart and his sister, Estelle Axton. When its doors opened, local talent walked in

*Stax Records*

and made "sweet soul music" featuring Rufus Thomas, Carla Thomas, Isaac Hayes, David Porter, Booker T. Jones, Stephen Cropper, Eddie Floyd, the Mar-Keys, the Bar-Kays, Albert King, and many others. Its staff was integrated from day one and even in a completely segregated society, they made music for a waiting, hungry and mixed audience.

**1959 - Memphis State University**, now the University of Memphis, admitted its first Black students on September 18, 1959. These courageous students endured many acts of disrespect but kept their focus and became successful graduates and outstanding citizens of Memphis and the nation. On September 18, 2019, five of those "Memphis State- 8", Luther McClellan, LeVerne Kneeland Jones, Ralph Prater, Bertha Rogers Looney, and John Simpson were honored again in

*The Memphis State - 8, in 1959*

2019 by the University of Memphis for their historic enrollment in and contributions to the University. (Three members, Eleanor Gandy, Sammie Jones, and Blakney Love are deceased.)

*W. C. Handy Statue*

**1959 - Ardent Studios** was founded by John Fry in his family garage in Memphis. Ardent became a major player in the development of the "Memphis Sound."

**1960 - The W. C. Handy Statue** was dedicated on May 1, 1960, in the W. C. Handy Park on Beale Street. The legendary Mahalia Jackson performed, and Lieutenant George W. Lee served as Master of Ceremony.

**1960 - LeMoyne and Owen College**s were colleges for African American students only and located in South Memphis. Some of the students attending these colleges who joined the National Sit-in Movement which began in Greensboro, North Carolina, were Earnestine Lee, a Junior at LeMoyne College along with five of her younger sisters, Brenda Lee, Ruth Lee, Joan Lee, Peggy Lee, and Susan Lee. They sparked great controversy by picketing downtown department stores. They picketed 17 times and were arrested 17 times. They became known as being the most arrested family in the entire nation for their involvement in the Movement. Some of the other students participated in the Movement by going to segregated lunch counters in downtown Memphis and demanding to be served. While still other students went to the Main Cossitt Public Library and the Peabody Public Library requesting to use the library facilities. All of these students were also arrested and taken to jail. Some of them were Rufus Sanders, Grace Meecham, Ed Smith, Joan Lee Nelson, Woodrow Miller and Marion Barry. These courageous college students participated in the sit-ins even at the risk of being kicked out of college and/or being barred from teaching in the Memphis Public School System. However, they prevailed, and their efforts were successful.

**1961 - Memphis City Schools** were integrated by admitting 13 first-grade African American students to previously all White schools. These pint-size warriors dealt a death blow to segregation in education in Memphis. The students were: Dwania Kyles, Sharon and Shelia Malone,

*Integrating Memphis City Schools*

Pamela Mayes, Joyce Bell, Clarence Williams, Deborah Ann Holt, Jacqueline Moore, Leandrew Wiggins, Alvin Freeman, E. C. Freeman, Leandrew Wiggins, Harry Williams and Michael Willis (now, Menelik Fombi.)

**1962 - St. Jude Children's Hospital** opened in Memphis. It was founded by Danny Thomas and managed by the American Lebanese Syrian Associated Charities. Today, children are treated for childhood diseases at no cost to their parents. The vision of Danny Thomas was

*Danny Thomas*

to treat every child without consideration of their race or ability to pay. Paul Williams, a celebrated Black architect, who refused compensation for his work, designed the first St. Jude Hospital building.

**1963** - This was the year that **Memphis State University** integrated the girls on-campus dorms. In the Fall of 1962, an African American female student registered at Memphis State University, was accepted into the University but was denied residency in Rawls Hall. She was told that she could only be assigned to a room with another African American student. This student, Norma B. Sanders and her parents had to make other arrangements for Norma to get to class every day as they lived in the then rural area of Frayser. When Norma began her sophomore year in 1963 at Memphis State, the school called and told her mother that another African American female student had applied to live at Rawls Hall.

Another student, Patricia Terrell, had been driving in to Memphis each day from Millington, Tennessee but her parents felt this drive was too lengthy for their young daughter to continue. So, the University contacted Norma's mother and informed her that another African- American female student had applied to Rawls Hall and the two of them could room together in the first on-campus dorm to be integrated.

**1963** - **Jesse H. Turner, Jr.,** son of Tri-State Bank President, Jesse H. Turner and Allegra Turner, was the first Black student to enroll in and attend Christian Brothers High School, making it the first integrated high school in Memphis, Tn. He graduated in 1967 and eventually succeeded his father as president of Tri-State Bank.

*Jesse H. Turner, Jr.*

**1964 - The 1964 Civil Rights Act** was passed by the United States Congress, outlawing segregation in America.

**1965 - The 1965 Voting Rights Act** was passed by the United States Congress, changing the political landscape of America.

**1965 - Miriam Sugarmon (DeCosta-Willis)** desegregated the faculty at Memphis State University as a Spanish language professor in the Romance Languages Department.

**1966 - Beale Street** was declared a **National Historic District** by the National Parks Service of the United States Department of Interior.

**1968 - Fame Records,** of Muscle-Shoals, Alabama, hired Earl Cage as a talent scout and set up a studio for demos on Bellevue Street in South Memphis. When asked, "Why go to Memphis?' Rick Hall said, "Stax cannot record all the talent in Memphis, it's too much for one label."

**1968 - Memphis Sanitation workers** went on strike and invited Dr. Martin Luther King, Jr. to come to Memphis to support them. He was assassinated and the Beale Street Project 1 was shelved, leaving Beale Street in shambles. After the riots of 1968, merchants fled to the suburbs, with many businesses moving to Park Avenue in the Orange Mound community.

*The Sanitation Workers' "I AM A MAN" demonstration.*

**1970 - The Community of Whitehaven** was annexed by the City of Memphis on January 1, 1970. Whitehaven was organized in 1871 and named after Colonel Francis White who was a major link between the cotton farmers of the Delta and the Memphis market.

**1970-73 - Beale Street** was reduced to rubble and hauled off to landfills. Over 400 of its substandard buildings were demolished, but several of its landmark buildings were spared, including First Baptist Beale Church, Old and New Daisy

*A deserted Beale Street landmark*

Theatres and the A. Schwab Department Store, among others.

**1972** - **Federal District Court Judge Robert McRae** ordered busing of students in Memphis as a major plank in the desegregation of Memphis City Schools. The plan called for some 13,789 students to be bused, causing "White Flight" from the Memphis School System.

**1972** - After serving as the first Black judge in Tennessee, appointed in 1962 by Governor Frank G. Clement, **Attorney Benjamin L. Hooks** was appointed to the Federal Communications Commission (FCC) by President Richard M. Nixon. During his tenure, Black ownership of radio and television stations reached unprecedented levels.

*Benjamin L. Hooks*

*The Memphis in May Festival*

**1972** - The concept for the development of the **Memphis in May** Festival was proposed by the Memphis Chamber of Commerce. George Brown, Rodney Barber, Harold Shaw, Sr., and Lyman Aldridge participated in the planning and discussion. Today, the Memphis in May International Festival can be proud of this initial committee and the movement to share the hospitality, bar-b-que, and Blues of Memphis with the world.

**1973** - **The City of Memphis** assumed ownership of **Beale Street** and requested bids to develop the historic street for tourism.

**1973** - **Federal Express Corporation**, a shipping giant, was founded by Fred Smith in Memphis. Although incorporated in Little Rock, Arkansas in 1971, Smith quickly moved operations to Memphis due to its strategic location and major airport, making it the company's headquarters and primary hub. Thousands of Memphians work at FedEx and many worthy causes benefit from the generosity of this good corporate neighbor.

**1973** - **The University of Tennessee Center for Health Sciences** (Medical School) launched a comprehensive Sickle Cell Anemia program for the Greater Mid-South to address the educational and medical needs of

Sickle Cell patients and families. Drs. Lemuel Diggs and Fred Krause led the research and patient care programs. Dr. LaSimba Gray led the community outreach program. When the program began, sickle cell patients only lived to be teenagers and young adults. Now, many live to be 60 years and older.

**1973** —Plans began for the construction of the **Downtown Memphis Pyramid** intended as a basketball arena to attract a professional basketball team to Memphis.

*The Pyramid*

**1974 - Harold Ford, Sr**. was elected to the United States Congress, having defeated the incumbent by 774 votes.

**1976 - Ruby Wilson** arrived in Memphis and soon made a name for herself in church circles, but her destiny was Beale Street. When Beale Street

*Ruby Wilson*

rose from the ashes of urban renewal, Ruby Wilson took her place on the stage of B. B. King's Club and sang herself into the hearts of its patrons. She was heralded as the "Queen of Beale Street," without debate. Her performances on Beale Street led to tours around the world, spreading the spirit of Blues and Beale Street. Before her death, she was invited by this author to participate in a concert, "Going Back to the Church." Ruby said, "LaSimba, I'll come and sing, but let's be clear, I never left the church."

(Please read, Beale Street Gumbo.)

**1976 - Main Street** was closed to vehicle traffic and opened as a Pedestrian Mall.

**1977 - WLOK, AM 1340,** was purchased by Art Gilliam, Jr. and became the first Black-owned radio station in Memphis. The format was changed to Gospel Music, Public Services and News. Today, it is still a "Family Tradition" radio station.

*Art Gilliam*

**1977** - The **Memphis in May International Festival** officially began, with Japan as its first honored country. Originally proposed by the Memphis Chamber of Commerce, the festival was developed by leaders including George H. Brown, Jr., Fred Smith, Harold Shaw, Rodney Barber, and Lyman Aldridge. It has since grown into a major cultural and economic event, promoting Memphis globally and generating millions for the local economy.

**1977 - The Turley Company** started developing housing in Downtown Memphis to reverse the flight to the suburbs. Henry Turley had a vision to revitalize abandoned vacant buildings in the downtown area, creating condos, apartments, and palatial homes on the banks of the Mississippi River. He was exactly right, "You build, and the people will come."

*Beale St. Music Festival*

**1977 - The First Beale Street Music Festival** was organized by Fred Ford, a saxophone player, and Jamile Nasser, a bassist. The original goal of the festival was to host a reunion of area musicians, Blues and Jazz from Memphis. Attorney Irvin Salky funded the festival with a personal contribution of $75,000.

**1978 - The Leadership Memphis** program was organized by Pitt Hyde, III, Kate Gooch, Fred Smith, Dr. Willie W. Herenton, Jack Belz and Sonja Walker to impact change for the advancement of Memphis and foster positive change and promote racial reconciliation in Memphis. The vision was to inform and train leadership for generations to come.

**1980 - Memphis Attorney George H. Brown, Jr.,** was appointed by Governor Lamar Alexander to the Tennessee Supreme Court to fill a vacancy caused by the death of Justice Joe Henry. This historic appointment made Attorney Brown the first Black to serve on the highest court in Tennessee.

**1980 - Attorney Odell Horton** was appointed a U. S. District Judge on May 12, becoming the first Black to serve on the Federal Bench in Memphis. Judge Horton later became the Chief Judge of the Western District of Tennessee in 1987 and served until 1995.

**1980 - Joe Savarin** organized the Blues Foundation to preserve and promote the Blues -- the music that made Memphis famous around the world.

**1982 - The Lorraine Motel**, the site of the assassination of Dr. Martin Luther King, Jr., was purchased out of foreclosure at a cost of $144,00. The movement to save the motel was led by D'Army Bailey, A. W. Willis, William "Bill" Adkins, Jack Belz and Charles Scruggs of radio station WDIA.

*The Lorraine Motel*

**1982- Memphis granted John Elkington** a 52-year lease on the Beale Street property to develop an entertainment district for Beale Street, and he did.

*Church Park Historic Marker*

**1983 - A Historic Marker** was placed on the site of **Church Park** to honor Robert R. Church Sr., by his daughter, Roberta Church, Ron Walter, historian, Dr. Charles Crawford, Richard Hackett, and the City of Memphis.

**1983 - Beale Street** was reopened, with fanfare, pomp and circumstance, as a major tourist attraction. As Memphis celebrates its Bicentennial, Beale Street is America's most iconic street, attracting millions of tourists annually from around the world.

**1986 - David and Yvonne Acey** founded **"Africa in April,"** an international celebration of African countries. The celebration is anchored on Beale Street in Church Park, with the mission of building economic opportunities between Memphis and Africa that are mutually beneficial.

**1988 - The Hein Park Historic Neighborhood** was placed on the United States Historic Register on November 16, 1988. The neighborhood was built between 1921-1941 on a former farm site owned and operated by the Hein, Mette and Gerber families. The architectural styles included, Twentieth Century Revival, Georgian Revival, Tudor Revival and English Country Cottage.

**1988 -** **The Cooper-Young Festival** was organized to preserve and revitalize one of the oldest communities in Memphis. The festival celebrates the vibrant local community with live music, art vendors, food, and cultural activities. In 2012, the American Planning Association cited Cooper-Young as one of the 10 best communities in the nation.

**1989 -** **Fred Jones,** a graduate of Booker T. Washington High School, founded the **Southern Heritage Football Classic,** initially featuring Jackson State University and Tennessee State University. The annual event has renewed interest

and support for Historical Black Colleges and Universities (HBCUs). The event has grown far beyond the football field. There are concerts, a parade, fashions shows, a golf tournament and tailgate parties that lasts for several days. The Southern Heritage Classic is the largest economic boost between Labor Day and Thanksgiving Day, hosting various HBCU teams.

**1990 -** **Lucy Yates Shaw** was appointed President and Chief Executive Officer of the MED, the Regional Medical Center and acute care hospital in Memphis. In this position, Lucy Shaw supervised 2800 employees and was responsible for a 200 million dollar annual budget.

*Lucy Yates Shaw*

**1991 -** **The National Civil Rights Museum** opened September 28th at the renovated **Lorraine Motel,** thanks to the vision of **D'Army Bailey, A. W. Willis, II, Charles Scruggs, and Pitt Hyde**. The Rev. Jesse Jackson and Ms. Rosa Parks, civil rights activist; Cybil Shephard, actress and local elected officials attended the grand event.

**1990 - Gray v. City of Memphis**, a federal lawsuit, ended the runoff in city mayoral elections. Federal Judge Jerome Turner ruled that the runoff violated the

theory of one man, one vote of the 1965 voting Rights Act. The ruling came in time for Dr. Willie Herenton to defeat Richard Hackett by 142 votes. Richard Hackett did not call for a recount.

*Gray v. City of Memphis*
*Plaintiffs Honored by City Council*

*Plaintiffs in the case were (front, l-r in the photo) Randy Wade, Rev. Melvin Wade, Gwen Sneed, Art Gilliam, Rev. Samuel B. Kyles, Dr. William "Bill" Adkins, and Dr. L. LaSimba M. Gray, Jr.*

**1991 - Dr. Willie W. Herenton** was elected as the first African American mayor of Memphis by a narrow margin of 142 votes. (Councilman J. O. Patteson, Jr. had served as interim Mayor in 1982.)

**1991 - Marc Cohn** released a recording, **"Walking in Memphis."** The song was inspired by a visit Cohn made to Beale Street, Graceland, and the Full Gospel Church of the Rev. Al Green.

*Willie W. Herenton*

**1992 -** Hollywood arrives in Memphis to film the movie, **"The Firm."** Paramount Pictures filmed scenes in the abandoned International Harvester Plant, the Cotton Exchange Building, the Peabody Hotel and Beale Street.

**1995 - Judge Bernice Donald** replaced Judge Odell Horton on the Federal Bench in Memphis, Tennessee, becoming the first African American woman to serve on the Federal Bench in Memphis. She later served in a senior status on the United States Court of Appeals for the Sixth Circuit.

*Herman Morris*

**1997 - Attorney Herman Morris, Jr.** was promoted to President and CEO of the Memphis Light Gas and Water Division. In this capacity, Morris supervised 2,700 employees and managed an annual budget of 1.4 billion dollars. This historic promotion made him the first African American to lead the Utility Division of Memphis City Government.

**2000 - Shelby State Community College** and State Technical Institute merged to form Southwest Community College.

**2001 - The Grizzles Professional Basketball** team claimed the Pyramid as its new home for professional basketball in Memphis.

**2004 - The Memphis Grizzles** relocated to the new FedEx Forum where they share home court advantage with the University of Memphis basketball team.

*AC Wharton*

**2002 - Attorney AC Wharton** was sworn in as the first African American elected Mayor of Shelby County. He would later be sworn in as Mayor of Memphis in 2009 and the first African American to serve as Mayor of both the City of Memphis and Shelby County.

**2005 - Walter Bailey, Judge D'Army Bailey, L. LaSimba Gray, Joseph Kyles and the Rev. Al Sharpton** called for the removal of the Nathan B. Forrest statute in a Memphis park.

**2014 - Claude Humphrey**, a graduate of Lester High School and Tennessee State University, was installed in the National Football Hall of Fame, becoming the only Memphian to receive this honor. He played 16 seasons with the Atlanta Falcons and the Philadelphia Eagles as a defensive end. He recorded 122 quarterback sacks, two safeties, was selected "All Pro" five times and participated in the "PRO-BOWL" six times. Dr. Keith Norman and the First Baptist Church-Broad Street dedicated the former site of the Lester School as the "Claude Humphrey Athletic Complex."

**2017 -** On Wednesday night, December 20, 2017, the **Nathan B. Forrest and other confederate statues** and symbols were removed from the Memphis landscape. Memphis Mayor Jim Strickland, and County Commissioner

Attorney Van Turner led the campaign to legally remove these symbols of a dark era for Memphis and the United States. The removal process had several chapters. In 2005, the Rev. Al Sharpton was brought to town for a public rally. Then, the Ku Klux Klan came to town from eight different states for a rally. Later, Sheriff Mark Luttrell assigned deputies to guard the homes of county commissioner Walter Bailey and D'Army Bailey, Dwight Montgomery, and Dr. LaSimba Gray. Still later, on the day of the rally, the KKK surrounded the park along with sheriff deputies and Memphis police officers. Prominent Activist, Tami Sawyer (who would later become a County Commissioner in 2018) continued the call for removal of the statues in the Spring and Summer of 2017, leading the #TakeEmDown901 movement to remove the statues.

*The Crosstown Concourse*

**2017 - The Crosstown Concourse** opened in the iconic Sears Roebuck and Company Tower. The building had been vacant for decades, but is now a bustling beehive of life, commerce, and entertainment, thanks to the vision of Todd Richardson and Christopher Miner.

**2018** - Memphis observed the **50th anniversary of the assassination of Dr. Martin Luther King, Jr.** as the nation focused on Memphis. Mayor Jim Strickland awarded a $50,000 tax free grant to each surviving 1968 Sanitation worker. The City Council added $20,000 to each grant.

**2018** - The City of Memphis established the **"I Am A Man Plaza"** adjacent to the historic Clayborn Temple AME Church building, and a **Dr. Martin L. King, Jr. Reflective Park** was established on B.B. King Street.

*The "I AM A MAN" Plaza*

**2019** - Memphis Mayor Jim Strickland hosted a Prayer Breakfast on January 1, 2019, and gave the State of Memphis Address and stated his vision for the future of Memphis.

**2019** - On May 22, Memphis kicked off the **Bicentennial Celebration, "200 Years of Soul,"** looking back 200 years and preparing for the next 100 years.

**2019** - On June 19, the city celebrated the **180th birthday of Robert R. Church, Sr.** with a parade led by Mayor Strickland down Beale Street.  It included live music and a cake-cutting ceremony in Church Park.

**2019** - On September 23, the television drama series, **Bluff City Law**, debuted as a Memphis-based courtroom drama on national television.  The shooting scenes included the legendary **4-Way Grill**, the National Civil Rights Museum, the D'Army Bailey Courthouse, the Walter Lee Bailey Criminal Justice Complex, Beale Street, and the lighted bridge crossing the Mississippi River.

**2019** - On October 3, **Mayor Jim Strickland** was re-elected Mayor of Memphis with a wide cross section of support.  The momentum for growth, grandeur and greatness shall continue in Memphis for the next four years and positively impact the future of Memphis poised on the American Nile -- the Mississippi River.

*Jim Strickland*

**2019** - On December 3, both the **University of Memphis football team and the University of Memphis basketball team** were ranked nationally in the separate NCAA sports polls for the first time in the history of the University. (See "The Role of Sports and Fan Avidity" in this volume.)

**2019** - Student Sit-In demonstrators observed 50 years since 109 Memphis State University students were arrested while demanding African American Studies and more African American professors and staff at Memphis State University.  Some of those arrested included student leaders David Acey, Marcia Brown, Janice Fullilove, Joyce Finley Fykes, Carolyn Miles Goodwin, James 'Deke' Pope, and others.

**2019** - The University of Memphis football team competed against Pennsylvania State University in the Cotton Bowl on December 28 in Dallas, Texas.  While they lost by a score of 53-39, the University of Memphis continues to improve its reputation as a Division I athletic program.

~ ~ ~ ~ ~

# Origin of the Blues

Tracing the origin of the Blues is not an exact science and there are no maps. History has not recorded the exact date or place of its origin. Neither has a specific person been identified as the originator. However, musicians agree that the Mississippi Delta is the geographical area where the Blues was born.

We know that in 1619, when the first enslaved Africans arrived in Jamestown, Virginia, they were not singing "The Thrill is Gone" nor "Stormy Monday." They moaned and groaned in their known dialect struggling to navigate the hills and hollows of the English language, but the enslaved created new means of communications. The drums had secret codes, the songs had hidden messages, and the dances ritualized and preserved their culture.

In the breaking of the enslaved Africans, original names were taboo, drums were monitored and denied, and common artifacts were destroyed. The enslaved were separated from each other by dialects. The breaking was not to Americanize the enslaved but to cause the slaves to become more manageable and dependent on their masters. The one art that could not be destroyed was the music of the enslaved. The crucible that gave the enslaved Africans "the Blues" was slavery— the perpetual pains of their inhumane treatment that legally lasted 344 years.

The first observations of Black music were in the hulls of slave ships and were later heard in the fields and worksites. The lead singer was called the "field hollerer." He or she would "line" the words of the song and the other workers would res pond by repeating them in the same melody.

*Crude homemade musical instruments*

This was an African tradition called "call and response." The songs were used to express feelings of various kinds. Most of the time, they were songs of sorrow and sadness. Then, there were songs of hope, joy, and inspiration. It is crucially important to note that the songs also communicated meetings and events.

However, the primary function of these songs was to vent frustrations and process their "blues." The songs of the field are impacted by religion and the church. It was the church that drew the line between the secular and the sacred. If the music did not appeal to God, praise or glorify God, it was the music of the devil. The church made it clear that secular music was not acceptable in Christian circles.

When the field hollerer emphasized God, Jesus, and the Holy Ghost, that was transportable to the home and church. If the hollerer emphasized raw human needs and grief from a broken relationship, abandonment, and disgust, that music could not be taken to the house nor the church. It was banned by parents and preachers. One of the prime examples was the situation between Howlin' Wolf and his mother. When he started to sing the blues, his mother made him leave her house and she never spoke to her son again. In one of his classic blues songs, Howlin Wolf laments this permanent separation:

*I have had my fun*
*If I don't get well no more*
*I have had my fun*
*If I don't get well no more*
*Oh my health is failing on me*
*Oh, yes I'm going down slow.*

*Please write my mama*
*Tell her the shape I'm in*
*Please write my mama*
*Tell her the shape I'm in*
*Tell her to pray for me*
*Forgive me for all my sins.*

*Howlin' Wolf*

The field hollerer who got saved in church often led the choir, congregational songs and became preachers. These strict enforcers of sanctification drove a wedge between the Blues and Gospel music.

Unfortunately, many talented singers and musicians were driven from the church because they wanted to use their God-given talent in the arena of entertainment, Tina Turner, Ma Rainey, Howlin' Wolf and Bessie Smith, to name a few. Those who ventured off into entertainment went at great cost but also into great rewards. Aretha Franklin, Sam Cooke, Ruby Wilson, and Carla Thomas never left the church. B.B. King, Howlin Wolf, Robert Johnson, Ma Rainey, and the like were not given choices – the church left them.

That tension between the secular and the sacred has always been an issue in Black Music. When B.B. King got started on Church Street in Indianola, Mississippi, the church said no to future appearances. When Dwight Gatemouth Moore returned to Memphis as a preacher, many church leaders were reluctant to receiving him.

What are the basic ingredients of the Blues? While there are many, the following are some of them: Anger, disappointment, pain, abandonment, grief, and frustration, without therapy (outlets). If only one source is to be considered, it is suffering. The suffering, in the Delta and rural life, and the second-c l a s s treatment for the African Americans, is the obstetrician that birthed the Blues.

The various plantation owners of the Delta had no interest in organizing this music nor in the training of the musicians. The musicians wandered from place-to-place seeking an opportunity to play, get paid and hone their skills.

Beale Street provided the runways, and the landing strips, for many of these soaring artists.

*The Ballard Jug Band*

# Metaphorical Language of the Blues/Beale Street

A metaphor, in its classical definition is a figure of speech in which a term is transferred from the object it ordinarily designates to an object it may designate only by implicit comparison, as in the phrase "dawn of life."

In the context of Blues and Beale Street, two factors must be considered: a) the culture that produced the Blues, and b) the culture of Beale Street. Therefore, many of the metaphors used by blues singers had their origin in the agricultural settings of the Mississippi Delta.

In the case of the culture that produced the Blues, there was a strong prohibition against education for the slaves. Slavery is at the ground floor of shaping the psyche of African Americans. Slaves were denied the use of their native language in America. For survival purposes, the enslaved had to close ranks and communicate largely with the lack of literacy. There were remnants of their native languages and when they associated bits and pieces of their African culture with their experiences in America, they created code terms and folklores by using their well-practiced oral tradition.

The folklore created during slavery preserved the history of the enslaved in the Motherland and in America. A vital part of the history included the psychological responses to the inhumane treatment of slavery. It was the psychological response to heartbreak, degradation and depression that fed directly into the lyrics of the Blues songs. Many of our celebrated blues singers could not read nor write but their photographic memory allowed them to express themselves playing and singing the blues.

On the matter of the culture of Beale Street, one must conduct a sociological survey of the patrons of Beale Street. While there was a tremendous mixture of ethnic groups on Beale Street, only the African Americans could authentically sing the blues. Beale Street provided a compact geographical area for the desperate, depressed, and determined people of the Delta and Greater Mid- South, to come and seek personhood. Beale Street listened and watched as the artists sang and danced to the melodies of the Blues.

A few of the Metaphors:

**Ace in the Hole** -- a hidden advantage.  Context: *"I keep a stash of money when times get tough, that's my ace in the hole."*

**Axe** – reference to a guitar.

**Axe** – being abruptly terminated.

Context: I'll stop by Pee Wee's and pick up my axe and meet you at the gig.

"Just playing my Axe" – Buddy Guy

**Back Door Man** – The secret lover of a married woman who escaped through the back door when the husband came home through the front door. Context: Howlin' Wolf in his song, I am a back door man. "When the rooster crow something tells me, I got to go!"

**Bag** – a reference to mental attitude that drives one to actions; what and why one does certain things. Context: James Brown recorded "Poppa's got a brand new bag." A New Attitude.

**Barrel House** – to party in a Barrel House joint where the patrons danced and drank whiskey out of a barrel.  Barrel House as a verb means to party while drinking whiskey from a barrel. Context: "Mr. Crump don't like it but we're gonna Barrel House anyhow"

**Boogie Woogie** – is the Blues sped up for dancing.  The piano is  the primary musical instrument. Context: Gate Mouth Moore song, "I'm your boogie woogie poppa and I'm boogie for your soul."

**Biscuit Roller** – a skilled lover that always satisfied his/her patron. Context: Robert Johnson, *"I rolled and tumbled and cried the whole night long. Boy, I woke up this morning my biscuit roller was gone."*

**Chitlin Circuit** – was a string of small night clubs, mostly owned by African Americans, that featured Blues and Rhythm and Blues musicians during the era of segregation. Compensation for playing often included a hot meal. Context: I am leaving Monday for a two-week tour of the chitlin circuit. "I'll cover North Mississippi, Southern Illinois and all of West Tennessee, all in one-night stands."

**Coming out of a Bag** – means going off on an opponent or venting utter frustration. Context: He came out of a foul bag I never expected.

**Chump** – is a weak individual that others easily exploit. Context: "He'll fall for anything; he ain't nothing but a chump."

**Chick** – is a good looking available young girl. She has sexual appeal and ignites the imagination of her lookers on. Context: The girl is shaped like a coca cola bottle; hot like red pepper and sweet like cherry wine. She's a fine chick.

**Cool** – an emotional state of calmness in a stressful situation. The person is grounded and has confidence in self. Context: He's always cool as a cucumber.

**Coffee** – is a description of a dark brown person just shy of being black. Context: "She is a coffee brown and leave nothing to be desired."

**Delta** – the elongated flatland between Memphis Tennessee and Vicksburg, Mississippi. Context: "The roots of the Blues can be found in the Delta of Mississippi."

**Dig it** – Do you understand it? Do you appreciate it? Context: I want to make you the happiest woman in the world.
Can you "dig it?"

**Doggin Me** – implies being mistreated in unfaithful behavior by a soul mate. Context: "I'm gonna leave town, if you don't stop doggin' me around."

**"Dust my Broom"** –   means split or I'm leaving. To break off a relationship. Context: Robert Johnson recorded in 1936 – *"I'm gonna get up in the morning and I believe I'll dust my broom."*

**The Eagle** – money in the hands of a baller or pay day compensation. Context: Bobby "Blue" Bland, *"The Eagle Flies on Friday and Saturday I go out to play."*

**Easy Rider** – a pimp or unfaithful lover. Context: Bessie Smith, *"Easy Rider, you see I'm going away. I won't be back until you change your ways."*

**"Hit the Pipe"** — to smoke dope. Context: "I'm gonna hit the pipe tonight." "Hit with a crazy stick" to be mentally off or crazy.  Context: "I believe in all my heart that boy was hit with a crazy stick."

**Policy Game** – was a crude illegal lottery that was conducted daily. The players would bet a set of numbers would be picked from the spinning of a wheel.  This is why policy is more commonly referred to as playing the numbers. Context: African American played the policy game to get ahead (economic)

"Have you played the numbers lately?"

**Rambling** - traveling or on the move. Context: Robert Johnson, "I got rambling on my mind, I got to leave my baby, because she treats me so unkind."

**"Spoon Full"** — a small amount (good quality) Context: Howling Wolf – *"It could be a spoonful of diamonds, could be a spoonful of gold. Just a  little spoon of your precious love will satisfy my soul."*

~ ~ ~ ~ ~

# The Blues and the Church

*East Trigg Baptist Church*

The success of the juke-joints, nightclubs, and cafes with dance floors was found in the therapeutic value of dancing. In these venues, there was freedom to move, pat your feet, clap your hands, or even release emotion driven screams. The ultimate response was to 'dance as if no one was watching.' (You were the dancer and you were your own choreographer.) One dance according to one's feelings, mood, or state of mind.

One of the earlier inspirations for W. C. Handy was the String Band in Cleveland, Mississippi, where the crowd danced to the soulful sounds of the music. Music that resonates with an audience creates or provokes movement. This is especially true with African Americans. The difference between most African Americans in worship and the worship of most European congregations makes the point. In the European American worship service, the atmosphere is quiet, calm, and serene. The experience is more cerebral than spiritual. In African American worship the experience is dialogical, participatory, and interactive. When the music reaches its crescendo, congregants are standing, clapping, and verbal in their praise. A deacon may stand and shout, 'Sho nuff!' A Mother feels free to take the isle and dance to the music of the worship. The call-and-response dynamic of African culture shows up in worship.

During the sermon, one hears repeatedly such responses as, 'Amen,' come on Rev, "I know that's right," and "Say it again." To the music there are rhythmic swaying, clapping and sing-a-longs. When the pastor speaks, or the choir sings, these words or music are often reflective of the listeners individual personal life struggle. Thus, responsive movements are ignited, such as clapping, moaning, shouting, and even the flowing of tears. It is believed that Sunday worship for many African

*Greater White Stone Baptist Church*

Americans became the place where it was acceptable to vent their frustrations of having to deal with the problematic situations in their lives, (i.e., racism, poverty, and being relegated to living a marginalized existence.) The powerful connection between music and dancing gave birth to the "Boogie Woogie Music," that was a form of the Blues designed for dancing. In a nutshell, Boogie Woogie music is Blues put to an up-tempo beat.

For years the Black Church, in many denominations felt that Blues was the music of the 'devil' and dancing was in partnership with this 'sinful' recreation. This erroneous association suppressed one of the most dynamic dimensions of worship, dancing. David, King of Israel in II Samuel 6:14, "danced before the Lord with all his might, wearing a priestly Tunic." When David's wife told him he had made a fool of himself and embarrassed her, David retorted, "I was dancing before the Lord who chose me above your father and family." David was dancing a praise to God for God making him King of Israel.

Studies conducted on liturgical dancing have documented the therapeutic value of dancing as a part of worship. Dr. Saritam Wilson, concluded, "Liturgical dancing has benefits beyond just including the creative art in worship. Those who participate report to have alleviated stress and worry." Dr. Wilson advocates liturgical dancing as a means of confronting depression.

Further, when the legendary Blues singer Gatemouth Moore returned to Memphis in the mid-1970's, as a gospel preacher, the debate among some church leaders persisted along the lines of secular versus sacred. The Reverend Gatemouth Moore was barred from many church pulpits and was looked down on, disdainfully, as that "Blues Singer!" Reverend Moore's retort to that criticism was, "I see the same crowd on Sunday morning that I saw on Saturday night," denoting hypocrisy! Dr. Benjamin Lawson Hooks weighed in on the matter and said, "As a suppressed people, we needed Saturday night and we needed Sunday morning, to survive."

*Dwight "Gatemouth" Moore*

*Mt Olive Cathedral CME Church, Memphis, Tennessee*

~ ~ ~

"If it were not for the Black Church, Black folk would have committed suicide."
**Dr. Otis Moss, Jr.**
**Cleveland, Ohio**

41

# The Metamorphosis of Beale Street

*Robertson Topp*

The birth of Beale Street is directly tied to the founding of South Memphis in 1846 by Robertson Topp. Topp arrived in Memphis with a vision of grandeur and tremendous wealth. When South Memphis was laid out, the main thoroughfare ran from the Mississippi River to the eastern edge of town. Associates suggested that the main thoroughfare should be named Topp Avenue. Robertson Topp refused the honor and named the main thoroughfare in honor of Edward F. Beale, an American military hero.

*Edward F. Beale*

Indirectly, Beale Street's origin is tied to the explosive growth of the steamboat industry of the 1850's. Beale Street Landing developed into a major port between New Orleans and St. Louis because of the steamboat.

The workers on the steamboats were known as roustabouts and stevedores. They were strong, muscular Black men who needed to unwind and relax after a hard day's work on the wharf. These men spent hours loading and unloading the steamboats. At the end of a work shift, they made their way up Beale Street to let off some steam and have some fun. As the number of steamboat workers increased, so did the number of cafes, restaurants, and juke joints on Beale Street. Beale Street became the locale to control this influx of Black workers. Blacks in general were not wanted on Main Street nor other commercial corridors of Memphis.

Nathan B. Forrest, while serving as Commissioner of Finance and city Alderman established the City Market on Beale Street at the corner of Beale and Hernando Streets. This was not a slave market and instantly became a gathering point for slaves between assignments and for Freedmen.

The placement of this market on Beale Street could have been a strategy to keep slaves and roustabouts from the markets on Main Street. The people would go to the market to make purchases, display talents, socialize, be entertained and communicate messages to relatives on different plantations or relatives working in different parts of the city. In the 1850's, there were impromptu concerts, jug bands, singers, children musicians and hustlers, in addition to pimps and prostitutes hanging out at the City Market on Beale Street.

Preston Lautebach, in his book, *"Beale Street Dynasty,"* suggested, "Those corners at Beale and Hernando Streets would form a nexus to Black culture and power for the ensuing century, a location unlike any place else in the world. (Nathan B.) Forrest had unwittingly placed the cornerstone for one of the most outstanding Black communities in the country."

The Beale Street culture was colorful, exciting, and could be dangerous, depending on the section. On the western end of Beale Street, there were merchants, businesses, pawn shops, and an increasing number of Freedmen. The sidewalks were lined with fruit stands, clothing racks, and the display of dry goods. The traffic was over-

*A Beale Street Merchant*

flowing and patrons learned to master walking on the cobble stones in the street.

From Second Street to Fourth Street, there were night clubs, cafes, theaters, saloons and professional offices of Black dentists, lawyers, newspapers, printing shops and restaurants. Pimps and prostitutes, pick pockets, and gamblers ruled and reigned. Churches and businesses developed in the mid-section; onward east of Wellington, now called Danny Thomas, were palatial homes built by the affluent of South Memphis. Robertson Topp built his house at Beale and Lauderdale Streets. The Hunt-Phelan Mansion was built on Beale, near Wellington. (The house is still standing.)

*Solvent Savings Bank
(Later, Tri-State Bank)*

*The Home of Robert R. Church, Sr.*

*The Church Billiard Hall*

*The Hunt-Phelan Mansion*

Robert R. Church, Sr., built his home at Lauderdale Street and Vance Avenue.

Robertson Topp laid the foundation, Robert R. Church organized the Black vote and wealth, musicians developed the tunes, W. C. Handy wrote the Blues, Lieutenant George W. Lee told The Beale Street Story, and the people of the world got the news; Memphis is the "Birthplace of the Blues."

~ ~ ~ ~ ~

# BEALE STREET GUMBO

The interesting thing about gumbo is although it has many ingredients, no ingredient loses its identity. Each ingredient contributes greatly to the taste of the gumbo. So, as it was, and is, on Beale Street.

On Beale Street, the many ethnic groups brought their culture and customs to the mix. The Jewish immigrants arrived on Beale Street to sell dry goods and farming supplies. The Italians came and set up markets and went to the suburbs and developed truck farms to grow and sell produce. The Italians had a flare for restaurants, theaters, and brothels. From Main Street to Second Street the Italians had fruit stands that lined the sidewalks. They were known for fine clothes and tailor shops. They made suits for men and sold women fancy dresses. The Greeks set up restaurants and saloons. The Chinese set up laundries and restaurants. The Irish gained control of Law Enforcement and kept the peace. German immigrants set up department stores and drug stores. African Americans brought their dreams, music, labor, and aspirations for a better life.

From Main Street to Third Street there were pawn shops, cafes, business offices, studios, music schools, doctor and dentist offices, and printing shops owned by Blacks. The farther east one walked, the spicier the gumbo became. When people passed Hernando Street they entered the Red Light district. Prostitutes walked the street, voodoo doctors and gamblers made their presence known. Pickpockets were many and swindlers had a con game going from sundown to sunup. Bar-B-Que stands punctuated the atmosphere and filled the air with hickory smoked pork shoulder and ribs. Chitterlings were cooked on open stands to allow the aroma to advertise the goodness of "Chicago wrinkles" and hot sauce. Street musicians competed for coins and voodoo practitioners sold their shams to desperate individuals. The policy games were in full force and people played the numbers. Dice games led to many deaths on Beale so much so that David P. Hadden, a city Judge, created a gambling horn to decrease disputes, fights, and killings. Dr. H. H. Johnson located his clinic on Vance Avenue in order to gain close proximity to the cuttings, stabbings, and morbidity that plagued touring Black artists. In many instances Dr. Johnson's office was the emergency room for Beale Street. He was known as the doctor of Beale Street and the physician for the Black stars and performers.

On Beale Street, it was the music that held everything together. Not just any type of music but the blues held it together. The blues made its mark on Beale Street via the jug bands, the street musicians, in the cafes and clubs, the juke joints, the theatres, and the saloons.

The following persons and personalities, as ingredients to the recipe, were the main ingredients that made up the Beale Street Gumbo.

## The First Five Ingredients:

*Robertson Topp*

*George W. Lee*

Robertson Topp was the founder of South Memphis, of which Beale Street was a major thoroughfare. Topp was the architect of Beale Street and named it in honor of General Edward F. Beale. Robert R. Church, Sr. provided financial stability and an entrepreneurial spirit. Robert R. Church, Jr. provided political savvy.

George W. Lee provided the business, salesmanship and the eloquence to tell the story of Beale Street.

W.C. Handy wrote the music of Beale Street and marketed it to the world. He became wealthy and Beale Street became famous. Robinson Topp set the tone for an inclusive atmosphere on Beale Street.

*Robert R. Church, Sr.*

*Robert R. Church, Jr.*

While Topp was well respected in Memphis, he was not popular with the masses. He was pro-United States and opposed secession. He loved the South but loved his country the more. He warned that a war between the States would devastate the South and recovery would be long and costly. He never pandered to the bigotry and prejudices of the masses. He used his eloquence as a lawyer and the logic of a scholar to publicly denounce bigotry as a deterrent to the intellectual and moral advancement of Memphis. His speeches were well structured but not well received by the public.

**Racial Tolerance:** The laws of Jim Crow were not stringently enforced on Beale Street as these Laws would have assuredly been an inhibitor to the ethnic mixture on Beale Street. Thus, people of all ethnic persuasions lived and worked together on and around Beale Street.

**Integrated Communities:** Robertson Topp built his family mansion on Beale Street at the corner of Lauderdale and Beale and had no problems with neighbors of African descent or any other ethnic groups. The Hunt-Phelan Mansion was built on Beale Street within the same block

*Hunt-Phelan Mansion*

Robert R. Church, Jr and Sr, built homes a few blocks south of the Topp's home at the corner of Lauderdale and Vance. U. S. Senator Kenneth McKellar lived a few doors south of Robert R. Church, Sr. and Jr. Blacks and Whites lived as neighbors on and around Beale Street when Memphis was segregated.

The Springdale community in North Memphis had a published and enforced covenant that restricted residents to Whites only. This was the case for most neighborhoods in Memphis but not so on Beale Street, which was in South Memphis during the 1840's and 1850's.

When Robertson Topp sold lots and planned the layout for south Memphis, he was only concerned with advancing the area intellectually and morally. On Beale Street, as immigration took place, the Greeks, Italians, Jewish merchants, Irish workers, and Chinese came to join the growing numbers of African Americans who had found a safehaven from the rural life and slavery. Beale Street provided the cocoon for personhood and a place to fulfill dreams and aspirations. Thanks to Robertson Topp, Beale Street became a microcosm of the world.

**Music, the Okra to the Gumbo:** The Okra of the Beale Street Gumbo is realized in the musicians who came to Memphis to find work and landed on Beale Street to play their music. The songs and music that started in the cotton fields and on the levees of the Delta found a home on Beale Street. Before the clubs and cafes were founded, the musicians and roustabouts gathered at the Memphis Market on Beale Street and on street corners. The Memphis market benefitted from the gatherings and allowed street musicians, jug bands, and street entertainers to display their talents. The clubs and cafes preceded the theaters and formed the major depot for the 'Chitlin' Circuit' for Black musicians following the civil war and particularly the second world war.

The exodus from the 'fields to the factories' took place between 1916-1970, the blues music was transported to the northern urban centers. Places such as Chicago, St. Louis, Cleveland, Ohio, Detroit, Indianapolis, Indiana, and many other industrial cities in the north were the beneficiaries of this blues music. Memphis, however, became a major stop along the way. Many Black migrants headed to Chicago never made it there. It was said that one night on Beale Street was enough time to develop the 'Beale Street Itch.'

When W. C. Handy arrived on Beale Street in 1905, there were bands, music schools and instructors already there. Men and women were eager to give lessons in music, but no one had ever composed this special music as sheet music. The musical seed that had been planted in Clarksdale, Mississippi, as Handy observed a small band play, germinated on Beale Street and he became known as the 'Father of The Blues.'

Virtillo Maffei, aka Pee Wee, owned a saloon that became the musician's headquarters on Beale Street. Musicians could rent an instrument from Pee Wee until they could purchase their own. Pee Wee also provided a central phone number for persons wanting to hire musicians.

*W. C. Handy*

## The Amateur Night at the Palace Theater:

The amateur night at the Palace Theater drew large crowds featuring aspiring artists on Tuesday nights.    The legendary Nat D. Williams served as master of ceremonies. Rufus Thomas was the "Lord High Executioner. "When the audience booed a performer, Rufus would rush out on the stage and shoot the performer with his pearl handled pistol loaded with blanks. The audience would burst into laughter.

*Nat D. Williams*

The amateurs competed for $5, $3, and $2 as prize money. Anselmo Barrasso, owner of the Palace Theater had a tender heart for children and often admitted some children without the required admission fee. B.B. King and Bobby "Blue" Bland competed and won most often on the amateur show at the Palace.

*Rufus Thomas*

## Beale Street and Women

The least known and celebrated aspect of Beale Street is the nurturing reception Beale Streeters provided for women. During those times, it was not the norm for women to become professional entertainers or musicians outside of the Church. Many of the female stars of the blues arrived on Beale Street as children and young women. Laura "Little Bit" Dukes was singing and playing on Beale Street at the age of ten. She sang and performed for six decades. Evelyn "The Whip" Young, Saxophonist, was playing on Beale at the age of 14. Alberta Hunter was performing at the age of 14.

*Laura "Little Bit" Dukes & Band*

Lil Hardin, a music teacher from a middle-class Black family who hated the blues and saw this music as beneath her upbringing, rebelled against her family to become an entertainer.   In her rebellion, she left Fisk University, where she was a

*Lil Harding*

student, and traveled to Chicago. It was there in Chicago that she met and married Louis Armstrong.

Ma Rainey II, left home in Columbia, Tennessee and arrived in Memphis in 1928. She left home to sing the blues because her family too frowned on what they called the "devil's music." Ma Rainey II was a favorite on Beale Street for many years. She was also a Voo Doo Queen.

*Ma Rainey II*

Bessie Smith, the most popular female blues singer of the 1920's and 1930's, was known as the "Empress of the Blues." Julia Hooks, Lucie Campbell, and Lil Hardin were also music teachers on and around Beale Street.

Ruby Wilson is cited for single handedly reviving Beale Street after it reopened in 1983. Joyce Cobb still performs in Memphis singing blues, jazz, and country. Barbara Perry has a smooth silky voice, much like Nancy Wilson, and for years was a crowd pleaser in Memphis and on Beale Street.

The legendary performers emerged and changed the American culture directly and indirectly. Furry Lewis started as a six-year-old with a cigar box guitar. W. C. Handy heard Little Furry and purchased for him a real guitar. Furry Lewis would leave the street corners of Beale Street and would perform for national audiences on television and at major musical festivals in New York. B.B. King, the master, the chairman of the board, the king of the blues, took the blues from the Delta to all the world. B. B. King with his smooth soloing sounds on his electric guitar, took the blues to a young White generation when Bill the Szymczyk added strings to his album, "The Thrill Is Gone," in 1969.

*Furry Lewis*

*B. B. King*

~ ~ ~ ~ ~

Bobby Blue Bland, Little Milton, Bukka T. White, Roscoe Gordon, Dwight Arnold "Gatemouth" Moore, Gene "Bowlegs" Miller, Rufus Thomas,

*Ben Branch*

Peter "Memphis Slim" Chatman, John "Sleepy" Estes, T. Bone Walker, Chester "Howlin' Wolf" Barnett, Bill Harvey, Johnny Ace, Robert Henry, Sunbeam Mitchell, and Ben Branch, collectively helped shape the urban blues sound that emerged from Memphis.

*Bobby "Blue" Bland*

*Willie Mitchell*

*Little Milton*

*Rufus Thomas*

*Johnny Ace*

## The Spice

The Beale Street gumbo spice was made up of gambling, prostitution, the policy game, drinking, hustlers, pickpockets, con men, and the well-dressed pimps on parade. Added to this were the eccentric characters, dope pushers, conjure sellers (voodoo and mojo concoctions), and the crowds of spectators who just wanted to see, taste, and smell Beale Street.

*Ella Fitzgerald*

Th e Mid-Night Ramble (1930 - 1950) at the Palace Theater took place on Thursday nights and was for Whites only on Beale Street. The White Memphians were provided an opportunity to taste Beale Street without violating the Jim Crow Laws.

*The Palace Theater*

51

The audience was strictly White and the show performers were completely Black. While Cab Calloway, Count Basie, Duke Ellington, and Ella Fitzgerald were main attractions, these mega stars had to take second seat to the "Brown Skinned Models and chocolate chorus girls." Often during the shows, the manager had to block White men from rushing the stage. After a few drinks, many White men were resolved to get hands on those "pretty little brown thangs." Those who had their wives with them were more under control. Yet many a married White man had to answer to their wives when they got to their cars.

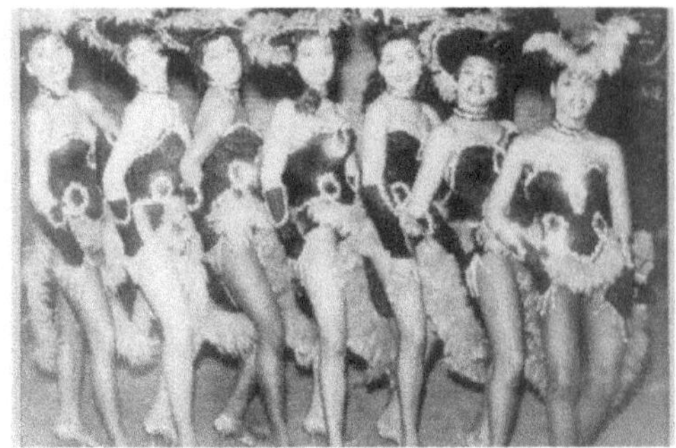

*Chocolate Chorus Girls*

## Shopping Opportunities:

There was an abundance of items that could be purchased on Beale Street. One could purchase products such as shoes, beautiful gowns, tailor-made clothes, handmade clothes and even hand-me-downs. Dry good stores sold everything from kitchenware to farming supplies and conjures. A most famous merchant on Beale Street, A. Schwab, whose shop remains a prominent fixture on Beale Street today, had a motto that read, "If A. Schwab ain't got it, you probably don't need it."

*A. Schwab General Store*

And so, it was in the hustle of the beginning days of Beale Street to the bustling of the heydays of Beale Street, a true and iconic locus in Memphis history as well as American history. There is so much more that could be told about Beale Street as each point of emphasis could compile a book filled with its own stories. What has been shared here is but a spoonful of an actual gumbo, evidencing itself as a metamorphic phenomenon of people, events, music, and a coming together in an actual development of humanity.

~ ~ ~ ~ ~

# Selected Famous and Notable Beale Street Characters

Beale Street is known for the "Birthplace of the Blues" and for placing Memphis on the World's Stage for entertainment. Beale Street is also known as the "Main Street of Black Life in America." But, Beale Street is not celebrated enough for being the only entertainment venue in the nation that embraced and mentored female performers. Women were drawn to Beale Street by their interest in music. They found their place as performers, along with the men on Beale Street because they could play there. Many of them arrived on Beale Street in their pre-teen years.

The patriots assured skeptical parents of their safety. Some came with parents, as in the case of Laura Dukes, and Alberta Hunter. Evelyn Young was allowed to play professionally on Beale Street only after her mother secured a chaperone. "Memphis Minnie" was only ten years of age when she claimed her corner and began to play on Beale Street for tips. Yet, in spite of their ages and gender, they were welcomed and nurtured to display their gifts along with the men of Music on Beale Street.

**Lou Barnes** — Lou Barnes was the owner of the Green Mansion, a brothel on Hernando Street. She was a tall mulatto with a great taste for pomp and circumstance and a flare for fashion. She was an avid fan of the racetrack and often attended with an entourage of glamorous women. The women were literally "Living Ads" for the Green Mansion! They wore fancy clothes, wide hats accented with large willow plumes, gorgeous gowns, and low-cut tops, and walked with advertising gates. Lou Barnes, without debate, was the most colorful figure on Beale Street in the "night life."

**Lucie Eddie Campbell** — Lucie Eddie Campbell-Williams was an African American composer and singer of hymns, an educator, and an advocate for civil rights. She was born on April 30, 1885, in Duckhill, Mississippi and grew up as one of seven children on the Byrell and Isabella Campbell family farm. She learned to play the piano by eavesdropping on her older sisters' piano lessons, since her parents could not afford piano lessons for her.

*Lucie Eddie Campbell*

Campbell was a graduate of Rust College (Bachelor of Science) in Holly Springs, Mississippi, and Tennessee State University (Master of Science) in Nashville, Tennessee, and in 1914, returned to teach at Booker T. Washington High School. She also worked with local churches in the Memphis area training choirs, promoting gospel music, training church musicians, and in the community as an advocate for justice and equality.

At the age of 19, she organized a group of musicians as the Music Club on Beale Street. She aspired to develop and polish the abundance of raw talent that she discovered there.

The inspiration for one of the most famous songs that she authored, "Something Within," resulted from a young boy that she observed playing his horn for coins on Beale Street. According to her, when the boy was told by an elderly man, "Son, if you want to make money on Beale Street you will have to play blues." The young boy responded, "Sir, I can't do that." When asked, "Why?" by the man, the young boy replied, "There is something within me that will not let me play the blues."

She was so impressed with the response of the young boy that when she arrived home, she sat down at her piano and began writing and singing...

> *"Something within that holdeth the rein,*
> *Something within that banishes pain,*
> *Something within me, Lord, that I cannot explain,*
> *All that I know is, there is something within..."*

**Black Carrie** — Black Carrie, was a tall shapely "brick-house" built dancer at the Monarch Club, a famous night spot known for gambling. Black Carrie had a way of clearing the dance floor with her hip swaying moves and sensuous gestures. The dancers on the wall would begin to stomp their feet and clap their hands in unison. Black Carrie was a "pro" at working the crowd. The patrons went wild and began to cheer Black Carrie on. *"Go on Carrie! Shake It! Ah Shake it, you ain't going to heaven no how."* One of her favorite songs to dance to was, St. Louis Blues. The crowds at the Monarch never got enough of Black Carrie.

**Two Gun Charley** — Two Gun Charley was the partner in crime with River George. Two Gun Charley was quick on the draw and a known marksman. River George and Two Gun Charley worked the steamboats during the day, but at nightfall, they made their way to Beale Street to raise hell. When River George was finally cornered in the Gayosa Lumber yard, Two Gun Charley was right at his side. The plan was to crash into the Shack, two men would wrestle River George to the ground, handcuff him and one man was assigned to cover Two Gun Charley. The two men assigned to River George were no match. When River George got his hands free, he went for his gun. The police officers fired their weapons. George fell to the floor and his last words were, "Charley, Charley, where are you? They got me Charley."

**Little Laura Dukes** — Little Laura Dukes was born into a musically inclined family in 1907. Her father Alex Dukes was the drummer for the Knights of Pythian's band that first played W.C. Handy's "Memphis Blues" in 1909. Laura was small in stature, 4'7" but equipped with a big voice. In addition to singing, she danced and played the mandolin, banjo, and ukulele. Alex Dukes expose

*Laura Dukes*

Laura to the music world by taking her with him on the road. She was often featured in taverns and theaters as "Little Bit." She performed and recorded the Blues around and on Beale Street for six decades. She died in 1992 at the age of 85.

**River George** — River George arrived in Memphis in 1900 as a roustabout and fugitive wanted for murders in Holly Rock, Mississippi.

He terrorized Beale Street as a brawler, robber, escape artist and an expert gunman. River George was tall with bulging muscles and a physique that could not be ignored. He was notorious and feared in the Beale Street Mob culture. He had a reputation of breaking up crap games, taking all the money, shooting out the lights and slipping into the darkness as the police arrived. He eluded the police and to add mystique and challenge, he would leave notes and send messages to the police as to where and when he would strike again.

*Julia Hooks*

**Mrs. Julia Hooks** — Mrs. Julia Hooks was born in 1852 in Kentucky and became one of the most prominent musicians and a pioneer in social work in Memphis. In the 1880's Mrs. Hooks was active with the likes of Liszt Mullard Club and performed in Classical Musical concerts.  She served as a consultant to several churches because she was an expert on the organ and training/ directing choirs. Mrs. Hooks founded the Hooks Conservatory of Music on Beale Street which was located in the Solvent Bank and Trust Building. In addition to her musical interest, she had a profound passion for the underprivileged. She organized homes for the old and neglected and for orphaned African American children. When Mrs. Hooks died in 1942, she was affectionately known as the "Angel of Beale."

**Alberta Hunter** — Alberta Hunter was born in Memphis, on April 1, 1885, to Laura Peterson and Charles Hunter. Her mother was a maid in a Memphis brothel and her father was a pullman porter. She attended the old Grant School on Auction Street and often referred to Grant School as 'Auction School.' Her

*Alberta Hunter*

family was tumultuous and difficult to navigate. She dropped out of school at fifteen and left for Chicago when her mother married her second husband. Alberta realized early on she could sing and wanted a career as a singer. To escape the pain of Memphis, she sought refuge in a musical mecca for southerners — Chicago Illinois. There, she found work in boarding, houses and was able to keep a roof over her head as a maid. Her dream was to earn ten dollars a week as a singer but found six dollars a week was acceptable until she found work as a singer. Once Alberta was  settled in Chicago, her mother joined her in the "windy city."

Alberta was given a chance to fulfill her dream as a singer at Dago Frank's brothel. Her gift soon attracted sponsors and more polished performers willing to mentor the teenager from Memphis, Tennessee.

Alberta was discovered by Joseph Nathan "King" Oliver and was baptized into Jazz. She never completely left the Blues, for the blues was in her DNA. But Joeseph Oliver added to her repertoire and exposed her to legends like Louis Armstrong, Johnny Dobbs, and Lawrence Duhe.

It was at the Dreamland Ballroom that Alberta exceeded her dream of earning ten dollars per week, she was paid thirty-five dollars per week. It was from exposure at the Dreamland Ballroom that Alberta began to tour in Europe. In 1917, she began performing in Paris, France and London, England. The European experience was transforming, Alberta was treated as an artist and respected as a human being. She was greeted on stage and off stage with reverence and respect.

In the 1920's, Alberta began a prolific recording career. She started with the Black Swan record company that was founded by a fellow Memphian, Harry Pace. When her mother died in 1957, Alberta created for herself a high school diploma, lowered her age and enrolled in nursing school. Then, for the next twenty years, Alberta worked in health care in Roosevelt Island's Goldwater Memorial Hospital.

When her employers discovered that Alberta had reached the age of mandatory retirement, she was terminated because she was thought to be 70, when she was actually 82 years of age.

After eleven years of missing the stage and recording studios, Alberta Hunter returned to performing and recording. Alberta Hunter was inducted into the Blues Hall of Fame in 2011 and into the Memphis Music Hall of Fame in 2015. Alberta appeared on national television, international stages, and in saloons and night clubs for more than 50 years. Age did not matter; her audience never got enough of Alberta Hunter. The final curtain on the stellar life of this Memphian was closed on October 17, 1984, in Roosevelt Island, NY.

**Mordecai Johnson** — Mordecai Johnson was born January 4, 1891, in Paris, Tennessee. He was a son of the parsonage and followed his father, the Rev. Mordecai Wyatt Johnson into the gospel ministry. He began his journey of preparation at Roger Williams University in Nashville. He became attracted to the Howe Institute in Memphis because of Dr. T.O. Fuller. In Memphis, he worked at the Iroquois Café as a waiter and assistant manager. The Iroquois Café was located directly across the street from First Baptist Beale and the Legendary Church Park and Auditorium. His tenure in Memphis was a proverbial baptism into the Mystique of Beale Street Culture. *

He later transferred to Morehouse College where he was a member of the Glee Club, the Debate Team and Lettered in three sports. His field of study at Morehouse was economics. The engine of his mercurial rise to fame was always his oratorical skills rooted in preaching. He served as pastor of the First Baptist Church in Charleston, West Virginia. He was the featured preacher in the Annual National Baptist Convention, USA. In 1926, Mordecai Johnson was elected unanimously the eleventh President of the Howard University as its first African American President.

---

* The Mystique of the Beale Street Culture includes successful role models and impacting personalities of defiance and determination. In that culture stood Dr. Thomas O. Fuller—a scholar, pastor, and politician without peer in the 19th century—alongside institutions of learning and community leaders like Rev. Blair T. Hunt, Rev. T. Nightingale, and Rev. Henderson Morris. Beale Street was punctuated for 1.8 miles with businesses owned and operated by Negroes. When you combine the business acumen of Robert R. Church Sr., the musical genius of W.C. Handy, and the oratorical skills of Lt. George W. Lee, you witness a capsulated experience of African American striving—struggling to survive and succeed in a white America.

**Riley B. King, aka, BB King,** was born on a plantation between Itta Bena and Indianola, Mississippi on September 16, 1925. He grew up on a farm and, at the age of seven, he carried the workload of a grown man. He cut wood, slopped hogs, picked and chopped cotton and plowed with horses and mules. Later, on the Barnett Plantation, he was taught to drive a tractor.

Riley B. King went to church and school at the Elkhorn Church. He attended a sanctified Gospel Musical, joined the St. John Gospel Singers, and became the lead singer.

*B.B. King Band in Concert*

Riley was introduced to the guitar by a Pentecostal preacher, who taught him his first three cords on a Sears Roebuck Silvertone Guitar. At the age of 12, Blake Cartilage purchased Riley's first guitar for $15. Riley repaid the $15 and that is history. In 1941, Riley left Lexington to return to Kilmichael as a tractor driver. One day, at the close of work, Riley was rushing to go home and left a tractor running that later found to be badly damaged. Out of pure fear, he ran off to Memphis. Then, after six months of hiding out, he returned to Kilmichael and paid for the damaged tractor.

In 1946, Riley followed Bukka White to Memphis. He lived with Bukka and learned the ropes of the entertainment world. Bukka White taught the young Riley how to dress and play a certain style of blues music. Riley later worked to attend the many jam sessions to learn from the Beale Street Musicians. He was able to get hired at WDIA as a musician and disc jockey. It was at WDIA that Riley earned the name, "Beale Street Blues Boy." Riley would become famous as B.B. King. While at WDIA, he met 'T-Bone Walker,' who played an electric guitar. Then, B.B. King resolved to get one by any means necessary, short of stealing one. Riley King stayed at WDIA for five years while "moon lighting" as a musician.

Following the advice of Bukka White, Riley always dressed to impress. He learned about the amateur show on Beale Street and auditioned. He instantly became a star and won competitions many times. Rufus Thomas, as the host, had allowed Riley King to perform repeatedly. Riley commented on his numerous appearances, "I needed that dollar."

Early in his career, Riley had met Robert Henry, who would become his manager. Robert Henry arranged for Riley to play the "chitlin circuit" and eventually get a contract with Bullet Records in Nashville. In 1952, B.B. King covered Lowell Fulton's "Three O'clock Blues," and his career exploded. For more than 78 years, B.B. King (1937- 2015) made a difference in the music industry and life in general with his voice, his fingers, and Lucille, his famous guitar. He played his last note of life on May 14, 2015, in Las Vegas, Nevada.

## I'M A BLUES MAN: B.B. KING'S LAMENTATION

*"People, I've traveled for miles around*
*Seems like everbody wants to put me down*
*Because, I'm a Blues Man, but I tell you a good man*
*Understand?*

*I went down to the bus station, I looked at the wall*
*My money was too light, people, I couldn't go nowhere at all*
*See, I'm a blues man, but a good man,*
*Understand?*

*The burden that I carry, it's so heavy*
*It seems like ain't nobody in this great big world*
*That would help po me*
*Hey, but I'll be all right, people.*

*Just give me a break, good things come to those who wait.*
*I've been waiting a long time, people*
*I'm a blues man, but a good man*
*Understand?"*

B.B. King

Lt. George W. Lee

**Lt. George W. Lee** — Lt. George W. Lee was called the "Golden Throated Orator" of Beale Street, born near Indianola Mississippi in 1894, graduated from Alcorn College and found his way to Beale Street after World War II. He earned the title Lieutenant from two perspectives. He completed officer training in the U.S. Army at Fort Des Moines, Iowa and served in the 92nd infantry division in France and received commendations for bravery.

Secondly, George W. Lee, was a faithful lieutenant to Robert "Bob" Church, Jr., the political Boss and Tycoon of Beale Street from 1916 to 1952. Lt. George W. Lee authored several books; "Beale Street: Where the Blues Began" in 1934, "River George" and "Beale Street at Sundown" in 1937 and 1942, respectively. Lt. Lee died in an automobile accident in Memphis in 1976.

**Tom Lee** — Tom Lee, a Memphis hero who, on May 8, 1925, was in the right place at the right time. He was passing the steamboat Norman on the Mississippi River near Memphis in the night. He noticed the steamboat was unusually tilted to the right side. He kept an eye on the steamboat and when he saw it sinking, he turned around and opened his throttle as wide as possible. When he arrived at the steamboat site, he only 
Tom Lee
saw the heads of passengers bobbing above the water. At great risk to his own life, Tom Lee loaded as many passengers as his small motorboat could carry and headed to the banks of the Mississippi River.

He reported to the *Commercial Appeal* that he did not stop to count the times he returned to the river to save passengers. He didn't have the time. When Tom Lee completed his search, he had saved the lives of thirty-two White people. The City of Memphis later honored Tom Lee by naming a park at the foot of Beale Street and a swimming pool in North Memphis in his honor. On the monument in Tom Lee Park, he was eulogized as a "worthy Negro."

**Memphis Minnie** — Memphis Minnie - born Lizzie Douglas in Algiers, Louisiana in 1897. In 1907, she began playing her banjo and guitar on Beale Street for coins. She was recognized as "Kid Douglas." In 1929 Lizzie was discovered by a talent scout for Columbia Records and went on to record over 100 songs during her thirty-year career. One could not hear her and not be impressed. Her songs included: "Joe Louis Street," "Boy Friend Blues," "Fishing Blues," "Hoo-doo Lady," "Nothing in Rambling" and many others.

*Memphis Minnie*

**Andrew "Sunbeam" Mitchell** — Andrew "Sunbeam" Mitchell and his wife Earnestine, operated the Club Handy and the Mitchell Hotel at 209 Beale Street above the Pantaze Drug Store. The third floor housed the hotel and the Club Handy was on the second floor. Club Handy was a major depot on the "Chitlin Circuit" from 1945 to 1958. The Mitchell Hotel was rated as the leading colored hotel in Memphis.

*B. B. King & "Sunbeam" Mitchell*

There, Sunbeam would exchange performances for room and board. Many struggling African American musicians stopped at Club Handy and Club Paradise to get a hand up. Chilli was a staple. He was forced to relocate his operations in 1965. When bull dozers began to roll, he found a spot at 645 E. Georgia and opened the "Club Paradise."

The Club became known for booking headline acts, the likes of Ike and Tina Turner, Nat King Cole, Count Basie, Muddy Waters, Little Richard, Elvis Presley, Howlin' Wolf and B.B. King. Mitchell ran night spots in Memphis for 40 years, housing, feeding, and paying Black entertainers who had no options but the Chitlin Circuit."

He was born on July 1, 1906 in Memphis and died in 1989.

**Will Self (aka, Dr. Scissors)** — Will Self (aka, Dr. Scissors) was a master of concoctions and voodoo. This practice of voodoo and witchcraft (doctors) had a direct connection to the culture of Western Africa where superstitions played a major role in African societies. The houses for medical persons were dingy huts decorated with "luck bags," concoctions brewing, and candles burning to provide a décor of mystique. Because of desperation and belief in many different superstitions of the Beale Street population, the occult was a prosperous business. (A. Schwab dry goods store sells the paraphernalia for witchcraft and voodoo even to this day.)

*Bessie Smith*

**Bessie Smith** — Bessie Smith, born in Chattanooga, Tennessee in 1894, found her way to Beale Street earning the title; "The Empress of the Blues." She became a major attraction on Beale Street in the 1920's and 30's. She signed with Columbia Records and recorded W.C. Handy's "St. Louis Blues" and "Gimme Pig Foot (and a Bottle of Beer)." Her ascending star fell into a fatal Mississippi descent in 1937 while on a trip to Clarksdale, from Memphis. She died in a car accident.

**Dr. G.W. Smith** — Dr. G.W. Smith was indeed a medicine man, but of a totally different genre. He was a major dope dealer located at the corner of Beale and Hernando Streets. Dr. Smith had the charisma of a chameleon. In the daytime, he presented himself as a Negro; at night he became a Mexican, a White man or some other ethnic group. His clientele was mostly white. Addicts could subscribe to his medicine on the streets or in his office.

*Matthew Thornton*

**Matthew Thornton, Sr.** Matthew Thornton, Sr. was born in West Point, Mississippi in 1873 to enslaved parents. In 1887, Matthew Thornton moved to Memphis with his family. At an early age, he found work with Captain Charles B. Church in the Steamboat Industry. Captain Church, the father of Robert R. Church, Sr., recognized the fast-learning skills of Matthew Thornton promoted him to coachman. Matthew was educated in the Memphis City Schools System and developed a strong interest in music. He learned to play the violin and cornet. He would evolve to organize the Knights of Pythians Band and invited W.C. Handy to Memphis to train and direct his band.

Handy would become famous for the Blues.

Matthew Thornton was somewhat of a renaissance man; he had many talents and many professions — barbering, musician, police officer, postal worker, and politician.

In 1938, Matthew Thornton was voted in a popularity contest to become the first honorary "Mayor of Beale Street, Matthew Thornton maintained the title until his death in 1963.

**Pee Wee** — Pee Wee arrived on Beale Street in the 1880's literally with one thin dime in his pocket. He walked up on a dice game and faded the shooter. He placed all he had on a Negro crap shooter he had never seen before. From that moment, Pee Wee was in on Beale Street. He won enough money to buy a hot meal, get a hot bath and sleep in a warm bed. The next day, still with money in his pocket, he walked Beale Street, got a haircut, and surveyed the landscape of the "Main Street for Negro Life in America."

Within a 30-day span of time, Pee Wee emerged as a well-dressed Italian man who had discovered his new home in America. Pee Wee made Beale Street his preference over all of the rest of Memphis. Pee Wee, though just 4'6 tall, was muscular and never backed down from a challenge in arm wrestling or large bets in dice games. To prove his abilities, he once betted he could swim across the Mississippi River or risk $1,000 or a single throw of the dice. Pee Wee became a legend on Beale Street, winning the respect of his peers and patrons.

In 1885, he opened his own saloon at 117 Beale. Through his challenges of the English language, he had a sign made up that simply stated, "P. Wee" The Pee Wee Saloon became the known hangout for struggling musicians, where he provided a phone number for musicians to receive calls and accept gigs. It was a safe bet that the most famous phone number on Beale Street was "2893." It rang many times for Beale Street musicians and singers.

*Pee Wee's Saloon Marker*

Pee Wee's Saloon, while managed by Lorenza Paccini, served as the headquarters for W.C. Handy's band. It was at Pee Wee's cigar stand that Handy wrote lyrics for visiting bands. Struggling musicians could visit the back room of Pee Wee's and select the musical instrument of choice for rental. This service was provided to give musicians a hands-up until they could purchase their own.

*Lorenza Paccini*

Pee Wee was known for his generosity in helping the downtrodden. He stayed open 24/7 and allowed patrons to camp out during the cold winter nights. It may well be that Pee Wee never forgot that group of Negro crap shooters who allowed him to play when he was down to his last dime.

*Washboard Sam*

**Washboard Sam** — Washboard Sam – aka, Robert Brown, the most famous blues washboard players in the days of Beale Street, was born on a farm in Arkansas and found his way to Memphis in the 1920s. When he arrived on Beale Street he met "Sleepy" John Estes of Brownsville, Tennessee and Hammie Dixon and began playing the Blues on Beale Street for tips.

In 1932, Washboard Sam relocated to Chicago and began a recording career. The unique sound of a washboard was sought by many Blues recording stars, including Memphis Slim, (also known as Peter Chatman), Ransom Knowling, Bukka White and Willie Lacey.

**Nat D. Williams** — was born on Beale Street in 1907. He broke the mold on traditional "Beale Streeters," he graduated high school and enrolled at Tennessee State University in Nashville. He earned bachelor's and master's degrees from Tennessee State. He returned to Memphis to teach at the legendary Booker T. Washington High School in 1930. He made history leap from the pages of the textbook. Students considered it an honor to be taught by Mr. Nat D. Williams. Some of his students who went on to fame and fortune included Rufus Thomas, Erma Clanton, Dr. Willie W. Herenton, Dr. Vasco Smith, Judge William Moore, Marion Berry, George H.

Brown Jr., and Dr. Benjamin L. Hooks.

In 1948, he was the mentor of Rufus Thomas and introduced Rufus to the management on Radio Station WDIA, where he was hired as a radio announcer.

Nat D. Williams was an at-large reporter for the *Memphis World* newspaper and hosted the legendary "Brown America Speaks," a weekly broadcast on WDIA. He also served as the Master of Ceremony for the Amateur Night on Beale Street at the old Palace Theatre.

*Nat D. Williams*

The Amateur night was a talent search and launching pad for the likes of B.B. King, Bobby "Blue" Bland, Laura Dukes, and Elvis Presley.

In 1931, the Memphis Cotton Merchants and power brokers decided to celebrate cotton to boost the economy. This effort evolved into the Cotton Carnival that would be celebrated annually in May. The Cotton Carnival included a series of parties, parades, and a royal pageantry featuring the king and queen who would reign over the celebration.

African Americans were left out and systematically excluded except to pull floats, load horses and to be on exhibition as servants and attendants to the royalty.

In 1935, Nat D. Williams collaborated with Dr. R.Q. Venson to organize the "Cotton Makers Jubilee." The Noble attempt was to include African Americans in a meaningful way in the celebration of the cotton industry. Nat. D. saw the necessity for such inclusion but recognized the irony of African American celebrating cotton, the commodity that locked the chains of slavery. To exclude African Americans was unacceptable.

Nat D. Williams was a crowd favorite for the annual celebration of the Cotton Makers Jubilee, especially the parades. The Cotton Carnival's parade was on the main street. The Cotton Maker's Jubilee parade was on Beale Street. The local high school bands participated, and the majorettes put on a show. Whites were given special seating in the bleachers and sat in great numbers to see the Brown cuties strut down Beale Street. Nat D. Williams died in 1983, leaving a large footprint in the sand of time and on Beale Street.

**Evelyn "The Whip" Young** — Evelyn "The Whip" Young was born in Memphis, March 25, 1928. She was introduced to instrumental music at Manassas High School. During her tenure at Manassas, she started out playing the clarinet with a group named, "Rhythm Bombers." She later switched to the saxophone. She was drawn to the saxophone and later mastered it with great vigor. She was able to turn professional at the tender age of 14. Her parents required chaperones as she started to accept gigs on Beale Street in 1942.

*Nat D. Williams Historic Marker*

She was baptized in the culture of Beale Street Music by the proven and best. She was a keen observer and learned to adapt her style of play to a given audience. She was known and celebrated for flamboyant presentations, the high energy, and musical innovations. She soon earned the nickname "the Whip" because of her vigor in playing.

The legendary Hank Crawford was greatly influenced by Evelyn Young and often on stage affirmed her influence. Rufus Thomas, the world's oldest teenager and recording star said, "She was a wonderful musician, plus she could sing." I was in awe of what she could play on that horn. Fred Ford, a fellow saxophonist commenting on the legacy of

*Evelyn "Whip" Young*

Evelyn said, "She was as fine a musician as you'll ever hear. She never got the recognition she deserved in her lifetime, but she could play with anyone."

Evelyn Young spent a restless three years at Philander Smith College in Little Rock, Arkansas. The magnetic pull of Beale Street and yearning to be on stage ended her collegiate career. In 1952, she returned to Memphis and joined the Bill Harvey Orchestra. As a saxophonist and associate director, Bill Harvey agreed to form the touring band for a new star of Beale Street by the name of Riley B.B.

King. Evelyn toured with this 21-piece band for eight years. B.B. King told Ms. Young on one occasion, "Everything you play on your horn is what I want to play on my guitar."

In the 1960's, she returned to Memphis and joined forces with Sunbeam Mitchell as his newly opened "Club Paradise." She became a club favorite at Blues Alley in 1978 as a member of the All Stars at the Living Room and Club Flamingo. She was a crowd favorite in the jam sessions whenever the musicians gathered after completing their gigs.

Ms. Young died October 2, 1990, at the young age of 62. Her life was celebrated at the Calvary Lutheran Church located at 1008 E. McLemore where she was a member. Her burial took place at the Calvary Cemetery and her memorial ID is 46764575. She accomplished many of her childhood dreams, however she lamented, "One of my dreams was to form a women's ensemble in Memphis. It may well be that the greatest tribute to Evelyn Young would be to form the Evelyn Young's Women's Ensemble on Beale Street.

~ ~ ~ ~ ~

# My Introduction to Beale Street

My introduction to the legendary Beale Street of Memphis took place in five stages. My father, the late, Rev. Leo M. Gray, Sr., took his boys, Leo Jr., Cleo, and Nacolis, to the "moving pictures" on a regular basis. We went to the Princess Theatre on Main Street and the New Daisy Theatre on Beale Street. We were required to enter through a side door and go to the balcony at the Princess Theatre on Main Street. At the age of 10, in 1956, I hired on to Mr. Buck's Crew to work the Cotton Carnival Parade on Main Street. At the end of our workday, we would walk down Beale Street to Fourth Street to be picked up by Mr. Buck. That work experience and my Eastward journey down Beale to Fourth Street in the Spring of 1956 impacted my life from adolescence throughout my senior years.

*Shainberg's Department Store*

In the summer of 1964, I worked at the Black and White Shainberg Department Store at the corner of Main and Gayoso. The Princess Theatre was located on the same block. Memories of the large fluffy malts constantly drew me to revisit the Princess Theatre. From the Princess I could see, hear, and smell Beale Street. Each opportunity afforded me, I walked up and down Beale, window shopping, eating the famous "Hot Dog Special" and the energy realized from the crowd and eccentric characters of Beale Street made every trip a transforming experience.

In the fall of 1964, I faced a crossroad. I had been awarded an athletic scholarship to Lane College in Jackson, Tennessee. Jackson, Tennessee was 80 miles away from home and I had never lived anywhere other than in Memphis, to my memory. Mr. Rush, my White supervisor at the department store was told by Mr. Otis Elder, a Black man who sold cardboard, that I had a chance to go to college and was not sure if I would go. Mr. Rush, about 5'7" and 135 pounds, got up in my face and told me in the most emphatic manner, "Leo if you don't go to college, I'll fire you. If you've got a chance to go to college you'd better go." I later learned from Harvey Tharp, a co-worker, that Mr. Rush was secretly married to a Black woman and was raising a mixed family in the shadow of segregation.

In the contemplation of my dilemma, I walked down to Church Park, and there, in the serenity of the "Garden for Gods," I resolved to go to Lane College.

At Lane College, I met students from all over the nation. Inevitably, when they learned I was from Memphis, they asked, "What is Beale Street like?" I took great pride in providing tours of Beale Street for classmates when they were in Memphis. We visited The Velvet Glove, The Blue Light Studios, Earnest Withers Photographer, Hooks Brothers Studio, the street characters, and all of the hot spots of entertainment.

Then in the early 70's, while attending an Operation Push Meeting at the Monumental Baptist Church, I met the legendary Rev. Gatemouth Moore. During the services, the pastor, Rev. Samuel "Billy" Kyles recognized Rev. Moore in the audience and invited him up to sing. When Rev. Moore opened his mouth to sing, "Jesus loves me!" I knew why he was called "Gatemouth." We immediately bonded, and he wanted to meet with young ministers. We went to the 4-Way Grill on Mississippi Avenue and my jaw dropping experience lasted for hours. He talked about his formative years on Beale Street. He had come to Memphis via a minstrel show and discovered the Blues. He remarked that, "When I learned that classic music wouldn't cut it on Beale Street, I had to learn how to sing the Blues."

During those early years, he had learned to sing the blues at the Palace Theatre from the best. He was tutored by authentic Beale Streeters who had found their way out of the cotton fields of the Mississippi Delta and the flat lands of Arkansas. Prior to this visit, he had been absent for decades from Memphis and Beale Street. He left because, according to his testimony, "It was too painful to stay. I had too many memories and heart breaks." This testimony was collaborated by Authur Cleaves, a neighbor. "In the heydays of Beale Street and Gatemouth Moore's zenith of fame, he had experienced a difficult marriage and many acts of unfaithfulness by his wife," commented Cleaves.

Gatemouth Moore recorded songs he had written out of his pain. One such song was, "Somebody's Got to Go." Its lyrics include, "Hey, Mr. Jones, turn up all them lights. My Baby's in this house with another man and I swear it's gonna be a fight. Somebody got to Go. It ain't none of me, but somebody got to Go. Woman, you done made me love you and you done made me your slave. If you don't treat me better, I'll be forced to put you in your grave."

In another classic Gatemouth song, he laments the brokenness of his marriage — *"Did you ever love a woman? Yes, and love her with all your might. And you knew it all the time that woman wasn't treating you right. Yes, you love that woman so much, she almost drives you mad. But you can't quit her, cause she had the best old something that you ever had. You fixed her breakfast in the morning. Stay home every day. You even wash the dishes when she has to go away. You send the children to school. You even mend her hose. You stay up all night with the babies and you wash her dirty clothes. But, when it's time to go to bed, that woman grabs you real tight, takes you in her arms and then squeezes you with all her might."*

*"She calls you a lot of sweet names and then you turn off the lights. That woman set your soul a fire and tells her baby everything is all right. That's why I love that woman, and I love her with all my might. You knew you could quit her, and all the times she wasn't treating you right."* I had to cry or sing. Most of my blues songs were personal experiences. I had to quit my wife and I chose to sing.

Gatemouth returned to Memphis as a preacher in 1974. Whenever he traveled through Memphis we would meet and we did what Rev. Kyles called, "Preacher Talk." He loved to visit Beale Street and eat at the 4-Way Grill. And he often told of his conversion from blues singer to gospel preacher.

~ ~ ~ ~ ~

# W. C. Handy:
# From Florence, Alabama to Beale Street

William Christopher Handy was born November 16, 1873, in Florence, Alabama, the son of Elizabeth and Charles Handy. Handy's father was the pastor of a small church and believed that musical instruments were the tools of the devil. Young Handy knew that in his Christian home there was no room for musical instruments.

Rev. Charles Handy, realizing the strong interest his son had in music, arranged for W.C. to take lessons on the organ. The organ was appropriate for Christians; however, the organ did not fulfill Handy's desire to create certain sounds. He secretly purchased a guitar, which was one of the many instruments he mastered. The clarinet became his instrument of choice when he was able to purchase one from a fellow band member.

The music Handy was greatly influenced by came from the church, the shovel brigades, and the sounds of nature. While working at the McNabb Funeral Home, Handy heard music in the sounds of grieving patrons and music created by workers as they beat their shovels against the iron buggies to pass the time. With a discerning ear, Handy could extract music from the sounds of life of the Southern Negro. Railroad workers could work in rhythm as a conditioned behavior after years of driving rail spikes and aligning rails. The workers of fields and levees discovered that their burdens seemed lighter when they could sing and moan in harmony. In these experiences, Handy found the raw materials for the music genre we now call the "Blues."

Handy was a well-trained musician. In fact, he was one of the best in the country at the turn of the 19th century. He taught instrumental music and trained singers in voice lessons. He was a professor of band and orchestra music. For years, W.C. Handy was on the faculty at Alabama State Normal School at Normal, Alabama.

His reputation spread quickly and demands for his expertise caused him to exit the halls of Academia.

When the call came for W. C. Handy to go to Clarksdale, Mississippi, he went there to train and conduct an orchestra for tourist attractions.

The migrations of Blacks to the North transported the music of the Mississippi Delta to Memphis and the urban centers of the Mid- West, namely, St. Louis, MO; Chicago, IL; Cleveland, OH; and Detroit, MI.

*W. C. Handy*

With the advent of the radio and the recording industries, the Blues became not only popular, but profitable. The recording industry realized a new market and unlimited materials and artists in the South. Also, the economics of the recording industry deemed it necessary to establish recording studios in the South.

In the 1920s, the Peabody Hotel housed a major recording company and W. C. Handy was called to polish groups for major performances and recordings. Matthew Thornton made such a call to Handy in 1905 to have Handy train the Knights of Pythians Band.

The call reached W.C. Handy in Cleveland, and off to Clarksdale, Mississippi he went. While in Cleveland, Handy had a "light bulb," moment when he observed a three-piece string band electrify a crowd at a dance. The crowd went wild at the slapping and stamping of a guitar, Mandolin, and bull fiddle. Handy listened intensely to discern the dynamics of this string band.

*The W. C. Handy Band at the Beale Avenue Auditorium*

# Danny Thomas and Beale Street

*Danny Thomas*

In the process of developing the Saint Jude Hospital in Memphis, Danny Thomas visited Beale Street and fell in love.  He contracted what W.C. Handy called the "Beale Street itch."

In 1931 by city ordinance, Beale Street was changed  to Beale Avenue. The ordinance required all roadways running East and West to be avenues and those running North  and South  remain streets.   Beale  Avenue  met  all the requirements of the city ordinance.

"Danny Thomas was mortified," according to the *Billboard Magazine*. When he heard of the change, he resolved to reverse that decision. In 1955, while raising funds for Saint Jude in Crump Stadium, Danny Thomas introduced his recording. "Bring Back our Beale Street." The crowd became ecstatic in approval. Mayor Frank Toby was in the audience and pledged that moment, "You'll get Beale Street back."

*Danny Thomas &*
*Mayor Frank Tobey*

The lyrics of Danny Thomas' lament were: "Wait a minute, (while listening to the musical intro), it's time to mourn.  Oh, nah, that's not sad enough." When the music reached the desired level of sadness, Thomas began to sing,

> *I woke up this morning*
> *Feeling mighty Blue*
> *Cause Beale Street isn't Beale Street,*
> *Its an Avenue*
> *Sweet Beale Street*
> *What have they done to you?*
> *I fell asleep on Beale Street*
> *woke up on Beale Avenue*
> *They say I'll get to liking it, if I try hard*

*Very hard*
*By the time I get to like it*
*They'll call it Boulevard.*
*Oh Sweet Beale Street tell me it ain't true*
*That I was born on Beale Street*
*To die on Beale Avenue*
*Now listen Mr. Mayor, I don't mean to be rough*
*The world is filled with Avenues*
*We really got enough*
*Oh Mr. Mayor I appeal to you.*
*Please give us back our Beale Street*
*Take back your Avenue.*
*Oh overall your propositions*
*May your fantasies stay unfurl*
*Memphis don't own Beale Street*
*It belongs to the world*
*Bring back our Beale Street*
*Take back your Avenue.*

Throughout Memphis and Shelby County, the song was loaded into Jukeboxes and a percentage of the revenue generated by spins of the record went to St. Jude Children's Hospital.

The lessons learned from Danny Thomas was, "You will never change a situation as long as you can tolerate the situation." Danny Thomas could not tolerate calling Beale Street, Beale Avenue.

**Ordinance #1518**, passed in 1931, when throughfares to be designated "streets" and "avenues" were clarified. Thoroughfares, more than twenty feet in width and more than two blocks long were to be designated as avenues if running East and West. And, thoroughfares running North and South would be designated streets. 1931, v 3253

~ ~ ~ ~ ~

# Selected Famous Quotes on Beale Street

*"A composite of colorful events."*   — W.C. Handy

*"Many cities make music, but no city breathes music quite like Memphis. The songs and sound that come from Memphis are uniquely American."*                — Shawn Amos

*"Memphis is a very lucky position on the map. Everything just gravitated to Memphis for Years."*   — Steve Cropper, Musician

*"The many sounds of Memphis shaped my early musical career and continue to be an inspiration to this day."*
— Justin Timberlake

*"I sang in church growing up. Memphis is the Blues Capital of the world, we like to say."*            — Justin Timberlake

*"I love Motown, but obviously always been more of a Memphis Soul Fan. If its Stax or Motown, I go Stax."*
— Justin Townes Earle

*"The Blues, very much like Gospel music, has a therapeutic value. Through both, pain and frustration are vented and processed. The only difference is, Gospel music is punctuated with hope. You merely vent in the Blues without hope."*            — L. LaSimba Gray

*"The Blues, the sound of a sinner on revival day."* — W.C. Handy

*"Blues is to Jazz what yeast is to bread, "without it, its flat."*
— Carmen McRae.

*"My father owned a pawn shop on Beale Street, the cultural nucleus of Memphis, which featured great local artists, traveling bands and musicians. In the seventies, A. Schwab's was the only store open on Beale Street. I couldn't stand by and watch such a historical street fall*

*into despair. I wanted to play a role in restoring Beale Street and honoring great Memphis musicians, because the city didn't recognize or respect them."*

— Attorney Irvin Salky

*"The blues tell a story. Every line of the blues has a meaning."*

— John Lee Hooker

*"Funk, gospel, blues are all out of slavery times, out of depression, out of sorrow."* — Nina Simone

*"The blues is an impulse to keep the painful details and episodes of a brutal experience alive in one's aching consciousness, to finger its jagged grain and to transcend it not by the consolation of philosophy but by squeezing from it a near tragic, near comic lyricism. As a form, the blues is an autobiographical chronicle of personal catastrophe exposed lyrically."* — Ralph Ellison

~ ~ ~ ~ ~

# Heroes for Social Justice
# Who Never Marched nor Picketed
# 1955-1981

Elvis Presley frequently visited Beale Street at the risk of being arrested under the laws of Jim Crow. He developed relationships with the Phineas Newborn Family and bouncers of various night clubs. The bouncers would allow Elvis to sit in the wings of the Auditorium near the exit in case a raid took place. Elvis did not go to the Flamingo Club to promote himself. He went to learn showmanship and how to control an audience.

*Elvis Presley*

He also went to Beale Street because that was where the music was that he wanted to sing. He sang at the Palace Theatre on amateur nights and appeared on the WDIA Goodwill Review. He had no reservations about appearing at a Black show for a Black cause with Black mega star B.B. King.

The late Dr. W. Herbert Brewster would often see Elvis in his audience at the East Trigg Baptist Church in South Memphis. When Dr. Brewster learned of Elvis' interest in gospel music, he gave him pertinent suggestions and tips. On the other hand, Elvis Presley helped many Black artists in the cross-over to larger audiences in the White culture by singing (covering) Black music. What Elvis learned on Beale Street, he took to the world. All of his hip-shaking moves came from Calvin Newborn, the Flying Guitar Player on Beale Street.

Dewey Phillips, the first disc-jockey to play Elvis Presley's recordings on air was also the first White disc-jockey to play Black music on a White radio station in Memphis. Black music was labeled "race music" and was taboo in the White community. Dewey also had the "Beale Street Itch." He simply could not stay away from the Black nightclubs and the Blues. He had no reservations about having Black artists perform live on his "Red, Hot

*Dewey Phillips*

and Blue" radio show and the people, Black and White, listened gladly.

Sputnik Monroe, a professional wrestler in Memphis who promoted himself as "235 pounds of twisted steel covered with sex appeal," marched to a different drummer also. He did not talk like a White boy, nor did he walk like a White boy. Sputnik had swagger in the early 60's. He strutted in defiance of the culture of segregation.

*Sputnik Monroe*

Once, when he was arrested for being on Beale Street drinking with Negroes in a night club, he hired civil rights attorney Russell Sugarmon to represent him in court. Attorney Sugarmon argued before Judge Beverly Boushe that Monroe had a constitutional right to go wherever he wanted to.

*Russell Sugarman*

The judge said, "I disagree with the constitution" and fined Monroe twenty-five dollars. Attorney Sugarmon asked Sputnik if he was going back to the night club. Monroe said, "If I don't, they win. I'll just take an extra twenty-five dollars to stay out of jail." Having Russell Sugarmon represent Monroe was the first time in Memphis history that a Black lawyer represented a White man in a court of law in Memphis.

In the wrestling culture, Monroe became the number one draw in Memphis wrestling. He was enemy number one of the establishment. Billy Wicks was the favorite of the "good guy" wrestlers. When Sputnik Monroe headed the card, seats sold out quickly. When Sputnik noticed and inquired as to why his Black fans were always in the nosebleed section of Ellis Auditorium, the promoters reminded him of the segregation law, "We can't mix the races."

But, Sputnik declared emphatically, "If Blacks can't sit on the main floor with Whites, I am through wrestling in Memphis." The promoters quickly realized the connection between Monroe and attendance—and they got the message. Monroe kept wrestling in Memphis, pinned Jim Crow to the mat and segregation was counted out. Thereafter, Blacks and Whites could sit together on the main floor during Memphis wrestling matches.

# 1968 — An Epic Year!

*The march of defiance and determination:* **I AM A MAN —** *1300 Black workers did not show up for work on February 12, 1968*

*"Something is happening in Memphis. Something is happening in our world."*
**Dr. Martin Luther King, Jr.
April 3, 1968**

*Tensions ran hot and violence erupted. Peaceful demonstrators were beaten by Police on March 26, 1968.*

### SIT-IN AT THE LIBRARY

On Saturday, March 19, 1960, several Owen and LeMoyne College students staged a sit-in at the Memphis Public Library's main building at Peabody and McLean. The group included Owen students Amanda Battles and Arthur Eberhardt, and Jean Wiggins of LeMoyne.

### ARRIVAL OF POLICEMEN

When the students refused to leave the main library, the librarians called the police, who told the students, "You cannot use the library. Go to the Vance Avenue Library (for Negroes)." These students included Clyde Battles (in the white sweater), Lucy Peterman (seated on the right), and Horace Bell.

### ARREST OF STUDENTS

After the peaceful sit-in at the main library, the students were arrested and put into paddy wagons by police officers. They were taken to jail, fingerprinted, photographed and placed in a large holding cell, where they were kept until midnight. Owen student Walter Wilson is on the left in the white coat.

### LAWYERS DEFEND STUDENTS

A battery of Black attorneys, that included, (left to right), S. A. Wilbun, B. F. Jones, A. W. Willis, B. L. Hooks, Russell Sugarmon and Odell Horton appeared before Judge Beverly Boushe to defend the students.

### OUTSIDE THE COURTROOM

Undaunted by their arrest and determined to continue the battle to desegregate public facilities, several students walked away from the courtroom after the judge's unjust decision against them.

*"What benefit is a leader if he does not devote his time, talent and wealth to the alleviation of poverty and misery and the elevation of his people?"*

**Ida B. Wells**

~ ~ ~

This admonition of Ida B. Wells inspired the philanthropy of Robert R. Church, Sr.  In addition to his wealth and power, Robert R. Church, Sr. was known for his generosity and endless support of the fight for equality and justice for African Americans, especially in Memphis, Tennessee.

~ ~ ~

*"We want the rights guaranteed by the infinite architect. For these rights we labor. For them we will die. We have gained one; the uniform is its badge. We want two or more boxes beside the cartridge box, the ballot and the jury box."*

**Sergeant Henry Maxwell,**
**Third Colored Artillery 1865**

~ ~ ~ ~ ~

# CHAIRMAN OF THE BOARD: B. B. KING
# 1925 - 2015

B. B. King was known and celebrated by peers as a gentle man at all times.  Bobby Blue Bland said on one occasion, "There is no need to try to compete with B. B.; he is the chairman of the board." Riley " B.

*B.B. King*

B." King came from a difficult, cold-hearted life on various plantations in the Mississippi Delta, but was never bitter about his past. At one time in his life, he felt abandoned and unloved.  He lamented in an interview, that he felt that his father loved him, but "He never verbalized his love to me."

Owners of the various "Chitlin' Circuit" joints, no matter how big or how small, repeatedly stated during his homegoing celebration in 2015 that, "B. B. never forgot where he came from."

These men and women had helped B. B become King of the Blues and after national fame and fortune, he felt obligated to return to the clubs and play, whether they could pay his fees or not. He returned to Itta Bena, Mississippi on a regular basis to say "Thanks" to those who gave him a hand up when things were really down.

In 1970, he won the Grammy Award for his song,
"The Thrill is Gone."
In 1980, he was inducted into the
Blues Hall of Fame.
In 1987, he was inducted into the
Rock and Roll Hall of Fame.

**RIP! Long live the "King of the Blues!"**

# Happy Birthday, Mr. Church

One hundred eighty (180) years ago, on June 18th in Holly Springs, Mississippi, Robert R. Church was born to a slave girl by the name of Emmeline and to Captain Charles B. Church. Captain Church owned and operated two of the most patronized steamboats on the Mississippi River that transported cargo and passengers between Memphis and New Orleans.

In 1851, Emmeline died, and Robert Church was sent to live with his father on the Mississippi River. The owner of Emmeline had pledged to her that Robert would never be sold to another owner of slaves. Sending Robert to his father was his intended passport to the North and the best education money could buy. Captain Church bonded with his son and decided to raise him and teach him the trade of the steamboat business. The relationship was nurturing and

*Robert R. Church, Sr.*

Robert served as an assistant to his father in many capacities, from errand boy to steward. The crew developed a pleasant nurturing relationship with Robert. Under the watchful eye of his father, Robert learned the principles of business with a special concentration in bookkeeping. Captain Church taught Robert to read and count receipts in French. Robert was a fast learner and listened intently to his father's instructions. "Be considerate of others, but always demand respect for self," admonished Captain Church to his son. He continued, "never allow anybody to call you a nigger."

This hands-on education and the eleven-year apprenticeship thoroughly prepared Robert for the tumultuous life he would face in the fast-growing river town called Memphis and the bustling street called Beale.

On June 6, 1862, the Civil War registered in Memphis in general, but on the Mississippi River in particular. The Federal Fleet arrived in the Memphis Harbor with cannons blasting. Robert Church was serving as steward of the Victoria. When the Victoria was overtaken by the Federal Troops, Robert was forced to make a decision, he could be captured by the federal troops, be killed or made a prisoner of war. With a splash, Robert jumped into the river and swam to the muddy banks of Memphis. The near capture by the Federal Fleet ended the career of Robert Church on the mighty Mississippi River.

Robert Church used his savings from his work on the river to enter business in Memphis. His first investments were in real estate and soon expanded to hotels, pool halls, brothels, saloons and ultimately a bank.

Soon after the Civil War ended, Memphis was consumed by the Yellow Fever Epidemic and racial tensions that lead to violence, death, and destruction. The White population, many with means to relocate, left in large numbers. Four days after the announcement that the plague was present in Memphis, twenty-five thousand (25,000) fled the city. Robert Church was able to acquire many abandoned properties further expanding his real estate holdings. Robert Church could have left in panic but never gave leaving a thought. He contributed generously to help Memphis recover.

African Americans remained and became 70% of the Memphis population in 1878. African Americans made up the overwhelming majority of the three thousand (3,000) nurses left to take care of the stricken. The entire workforce assigned by city officials to clean up the streets, bury the dead, clean up the dumps, drain the bayous, burn contaminated rags, and spread lime over the vacant lots were African Americans. These heroic efforts were performed with great risk in the true sense of altruism.

The Yellow Fever Epidemic of 1878 tremendously eroded the tax base and city coffers. Memphis was unable to service a five million dollar debt, adequately provide city services and pay State taxes. Memphis was stripped of the city charter and reduced to a mere taxing district in Tennessee. The Memphis that was founded in 1819 with great promise and potential was no more.

The State of Tennessee appointed Dr. D. T. Porter and David Hadden to provide leadership to the "taxing district on the bluff."

Under austere supervision and tight fiscal controls, Memphis began to rise from the ashes of devastation. Prominent citizens debated strategies to be relieved of the debt and restore Memphis to a city on the Bluff. In addition to discussions and debates, Memphis needed investors willing to take a chance on the future. The bond market was uncertain about the potential of Memphis

*Robert R. Church, Jr. and Associates, W. C. Handy and Lt. George W. Lee*

and citizens were reluctant to take a chance on Memphis. Robert R. Church remained bullish on Memphis.

In 1885, Robert R. Church purchased the first one-thousand-dollar municipal bond, and the dam of fear was broken. By the Summer of that year, local banks and wealthy individuals purchased more than $200,000 worth of bonds. Memphis accepted responsibility for the five-million-dollar debt and continued to rid the city of unsanitary conditions.

In 1891, the Tennessee State Legislature restored the charter and designation of a city. In 1893, Memphis was given taxing authority and home rule. This accomplishment may well be attributable to Robert R. Church for his courageous act of selflessness and his commitment to Memphis. The Evening Scimitar in 1899 published an editorial of Robert R. Church "...It may be said of Robert R. Church that his word is as good as his bond. No appeal to him for the aid of a charity or public enterprise for the benefit of Memphis has ever been in vain. He is for Memphis first, last and all the time..."

John Overton, Andrew Jackson, and James Winchester founded Memphis in 1819. It is safe to say, in1885, Robert R. Church, Sr. saved Memphis.

HAPPY BIRTHDAY MR. CHURCH AND THANKS A MILLION FOR MEMPHIS AND BEALE STREET!!!!!

Memphis celebrated the birth of Robert Reid Church, Sr. as a part of the Memphis Bicentennial on Tuesday, June 18, 2019, with a parade down Beale Street to Church Park. Mayor Jim Strickland issued a proclamation that was given to Ron Walter, General Manager of WREG TV and local historian. Mini speeches were given by Mayor Strickland, Jimmy Rout, historian for Shelby County, Elaine Turner, President of Heritage Tours, Roby Williams, President of Black Business Association of Memphis and Dr. David Acey, President of Africa in April. Music was provided by the Legendary Ms. Toni Green, local blues singer. Mayor Strickland cut the large birthday cake secured by Angelique Gray and good fellowship with all Memphians capped off the celebration.

The parade started at Beale and Second Steets, with Mayor Jim Strickland riding in the lead car driven by Maurice Woodard, President of the Strictly Vettes Club of Memphis.

~ ~ ~ ~ ~

# IF BEALE STREET COULD TALK

When I first heard  the promotional 2018 campaign for the movie, "If Beale Street Could Talk" I became excited and hopeful of revisiting the legendary Beale Street of Memphis. To my utter disappointment the movie has nothing to do with the 1.8 mile long street in Memphis.

The basic reason for my disappointment is rooted in my personal "Beale Street Experience." I was introduced to Beale Street by my father, the late Rev. Leo M. Gray, Sr. Periodically, he would take my two brothers and me to the New Daisy Theatre on Beale. When I asked why we were not going to the Princess on Main Street, he explained, "at the New Daisy we don't have to sit in the balcony, we can sit on the main floor."

In route to the New Daisy, we were enthralled by the carnival atmosphere, the aroma of soul food and the eccentric characters of Beale Street. The music pouring out of the juke joints and cafes was captivating. We felt the urge to walk with a bounce because of the bass guitar and drums—we had swagger before we knew what swagger was.

*New Daisy Theatre*

In 1956, "Mr. Buck," an African American entrepreneur, would hire boys from our neighborhood to work the Cotton Carnival Parade on Main

*The Cotton Carnival*

Street. Our assignment was to sell popcorn and cotton candy from Main and Poplar to Main and Beale. Mr. Buck would meet us halfway to collect the money and replenish our trays. When we reached Beale Street, we turned East and walked down to Fourth Street, where Mr. Buck would  pick us up.

The Beale Street Experience began the minute we turned on Beale. On Main Street, we could not walk on the sidewalk. On Main Street, we could not look White folk in the face as we sold them our goods. Mr. Buck was very stern as he taught the acceptable behavior for Main Street. We were to avoid prolonged encounters with White females. We were drilled on saying "Yes sir" and "No ma'am." To make sure we understood the gravity of the era, he would say, "Yall do remember Emmitt Till, don't you?"

On Beale Street we felt free to joke and play with each other. There was a feeling of newfound freedom. We could look people in their faces, we did not have to walk off the curbs in the street, we could pop our fingers to the hard-hitting Rhythm and Blues songs. We could partake of the hot dog specials, the sizzling hamburgers, chitterlings, and bar-b-que. On Beale Street, the Cotton Makers Jubilee Parade took place. We saw African Americans riding on floats and in fine decorated cars. What a contrast to Main Street!

Main Street had all White participants except for African Americans pulling floats or sweeping up behind the horses. On Beale Street, the Cotton Makers Jubilee Parade had all African Americans. The Marching bands of local high schools entered competition and with sonic sounds

*Cotton Makers Jubilee*

of music and high stepping majorettes, the audience was spellbound for hours at a time. The legendary Nat D. Williams, first radio personality at WDIA Radio station, kept the excitement by giving colorful commentary on every segment of the parade.

One could not forget the colorful characters of Beale Street and the men who wore coordinated suits, shoes and hats with processed hair; the curvaceous women who walked with advertising gaits and long eye lashes, the impromptu street concerts by bands and musicians, the "barkers" pleading for customers to enter their stores and shop, the shoeshine boys with their mobile shine parlors and the bustling crowds. Along the eastward journey, professional Blacks punctuated the landscape. There were lawyers, doctors, dentists, printing shops, photographers, banks, insurance companies, and benevolent organizations. Mr. Robert Morris was the manager of the New Daisy Theatre and my school principal.

When we reached Fourth Street, there was this magnificent, massive church: First Baptist Beale. The Church Park and Auditorium were on the east side of the church, and we could go into the park. This was revolutionary to me, for I lived across the street from Winchester Park, but we could not go into that park and enjoy the amenities of recreation.

*First Baptist Church*

When our ride showed up, we scampered to get on the truck and claim our seats. Mr. Buck would come around to each worker, collect money, and pay off for that day's work. My first experience on Beale Street far exceeded my compensation; Beale Street had given me a sense of "somebodiness." As we drove off, a sense of longing for more filled my spirit. From that day to now, I have loved Beale Street.

Through the annals of history, we realize that Beale Street does talk. The record is that Beale Street was a mecca for African Americans all over the South. The legendary Lt. George W. Lee stated, "Beale Street is a composite of colorful incidents." It was on Beale Street that Lt. Lee collaborated with W. C. Handy and Robert Church to make Beale Street the epic experience of African Americans. It was on Beale Street that W.C. Handy, father of the Blues, hearing the moans and groans of African Americans vented in song and dance, put pen to scale and the Blues was born. Beale Street was the venue of Robert Church, Sr., the first millionaire of African descent in the South. He controlled political patronage for the "negro" in the Mid-South from reconstruction through World War I. He was the go-to-person to mobilize the "negro vote" and to get a true reading of the temperament of the "negro." Robert Church, Sr. built a park and auditorium for his people when city fathers continued to make empty promises. In 1899, without a dime of tax money, Robert Church built a recreational oasis in the midst of the desert of segregation second to none. G. P. Hamilton in his book, "The Bright Side of Memphis" described Church Park as the most attractive park in Memphis, "lighted up at night, it looked like a fairy land or garden for the gods." While Church Park was developed for African Americans, it was open to all, regardless of race, creed, or national origin. President Theodore Roosevelt spoke in Church Park while Memphis was totally segregated.

Advocacy journalism was born on Beale Street. When W.E.B. Dubois partnered with Harry Pace to organize and publish the *Moon Magazine,* Ida B. Wells published the *Memphis Free Press* on Beale Street. Her motive was to expose the lynchings of African Americans and to end the bastard acts of violence. She was run out of town by daily threats on her life. She later emerged as a national leader and charter member of the National Association for the Advancement of Colored People (NAACP). In 1892, Dr. M.V. Lynk published the first medical journal for "Negro" physicians on Beale Street — *"The Medical and Surgical Observer."*

*Ida B. Wells*

Beale Street was an incubator for business development by and for African Americans. Universal Life Insurance Company, Hooks Brothers Photography, Robert Henry Promotions, and the Solvent Savings Bank of Memphis were just a few of the African American businesses on Beale Street.

Beale Street continues to invite the world to come and appreciate the struggles, contributions and accomplishments of a people who lived under the dark clouds of segregation and marginalization. It was on Beale Street that African Americans found a soul force to endure the pathos of a toxic society and the residue of slavery. That "Soul Force" is somebodiness and a positive self-regard.

She has gone through several stages of development, from the ashes of slavery to the crescendo of grandeur at the turn of the 20th Century. In the aftermath of the assassination of Dr. Martin L. King, Jr., in 1968, Beale Street was dealt a morbid wound by the concepts of Urban Renewal of the 1970's. Buildings were gutted and abandoned. The bustling crowds were diminished to a scarce few. The music stopped on Beale and relocated. When the legendary "Gatemouth Moore" visited his old stomping grounds in the early 70's he wrote a song, "Beale Street is gone and Beale Street ain't Beale Street no more." The kitchens were closed; lights were turned off and Memphis erroneously announced the death of Beale Street. In spite of the obituary of Beale the tourists kept coming and inquiring, "What happened to Beale Street?" Abe Schwab resolved to stay open and serve his loyal customer base. When asked why, he replied, "You have to understand Beale Street is more than a destination, Beale Street is an attitude."

The attitude of defiance and determination sustained Beale Street through her most challenging time. The City Leaders in many instances were like Pilot in the Bible, thinking Beale Street remained the stain of blood and by Urban Removal, the hands of power could be washed free of a martyr's blood. The essence of Beale Street was not just in the buildings; the essence of Beale Street was in the souls of all who drank from the refreshing waters of affirmation and transformation. That fountain was on Beale Street for African Americans of the Greater Mid- South.

Today, Beale Street stands with opened arms beckoning the world to come, see and taste "Soul."

Beale Street is too important to the history of African Americans and to Memphis to be trivialized in a movie title. The false expectations created by the movie title, "If Beale Street Could Talk," leads me to seriously propose to City Fathers and to all stakeholders that the brand "Beale Street" should be copyrighted immediately.

~ ~ ~ ~ ~

# The Role of Sports and Fan Avidity in the Transformation of Memphis

In the metamorphosis of Memphis, too often the role of sports and fan avidity are overlooked. Sports in Memphis have long been part of the City's social fabric — from The New Memphis Jockey Club in the 1800's on up to the University of Memphis football team's appearance in the 2019 Goodyear Cotton Bowl.

It was basketball in the 1960's in the Memphis City Schools that led to the integration and the easing of racial tensions. Bobby Smith was the leading high school basketball star with the Golden Wildcats at Melrose High School, a school for Black students only at that time. Wherever the Golden Wildcats played basketball in the city, the principals and athletic directors of the hosting schools were instructed to reserve seats for White fans.

*Bobby Smith*

The reserved seats were strategically positioned near an exit. The strategy was to provide a quick exit for Whites if the police showed up or if a fight or any confusion erupted. Jim Crow laws prohibited the mixing of the races for any public event. In the early 1960's, Memphis was still in the vice grip of segregation. It could well be said that Bobby 'Bingo' Smith integrated Memphis with a basketball.

Many of the White fans wanted Bobby Smith to attend Memphis State University and wear a Tiger basketball uniform. But to their dismay, the athletic officials at Memphis State had no interest in Bobby Smith. Then head basketball coach, Dean Echlers, tried unsuccessfully to recruit Bobby Smith. Reportedly, the Athletic Department officials denied the recruitment of Bobby Smith because he had made a low score on a university administered exam. The community did not accept that excuse. Bobby Smith was Black, and Memphis State University did not offer scholarships to Black athletes. Bobby Smith, however, was offered athletic scholarships at one hundred twenty-six colleges and universities. To their ecstatic delight, Bobby Smith chose and signed with the University of Tulsa. In 1966, Memphis State was on the schedule to play Tulsa University in basketball. When Memphis State hosted the Tulsa Hurricanes at the Mid-South Coliseum the next season, even though the game was a sellout, hundreds of fans showed up hoping to get a ticket. In that game, Bobby Smith was the leading scorer and Tulsa defeated Memphis State 80 to 63. "Bobby," according to Pete Mitchell, "put on a shooting exhibition." The Memphis State fan base, lamented, "Why did Memphis State allow Bobby to get away?"

The fan avidity of the Memphis State Tigers forced the administration to revisit its policy on Black student athletes. Later Herb Hilliard of Woodstock High School, also a school for Black students only at that time, was recruited and given an athletic scholarship in 1966. Much like Jackie Robinson for baseball, Hilliard was tapped because he was considered safe. He was a solid individual both in the classroom  and on the basketball court. Hilliard's contributions far exceeded his playing basketball; it was his pioneering presence in a Tiger uniform that led to the 'Athletic Dynasty' that Memphis State was to become.

*Herb Hilliard*

In the 1968-69 school year, Melrose High School produced another super star by the name of Larry Finch. Larry was highly recruited by major universities, including Tulsa University. Locally, the fan base of Melrose High School urged Larry to ignore the Memphis State offer. However, the fan base of Memphis State, lamenting how Bobby Smith had 'gotten away,' was urging the administration to sign Larry Finch.

*Larry Fitch*

The Black fan base, however, reminded Larry Finch of how cruelly Bobby Smith had been treated by Memphis State University. The cruelty was not just due to the fact that Memphis State did not welcome Black athletes, it was the cruelty of the recruiting process used to deny Black  athletes such as Bobby Smith. The civil rights community of Memphis saw Larry Finch as a bargaining chip to demand better conditions for Black students at Memphis State and to demand the addition of Black faculty members at Memphis State.

Leonard Draper, a major supporter and long-standing mentor for Larry Finch, weighed in on this controversy. Leonard Draper saw the bigger picture and used his long-standing relationship with Larry to persuade him to sign with Memphis State and become a Memphis State basketball Tiger. The opposition to Larry's decision was so severe that Larry's High School Coach, William Collins refused to attend the signing ceremony. Along with that, Leonard Draper received strong unfavorable criticism for his role in persuading Larry Finch to become a Memphis State basketball player.

*Leonard Draper*

Larry Finch was joined at Memphis State by Ronnie, Big Cat' 

*Larry Finch, Ronnie Robinson &
Larry Kenon*

Robinson. This dynamic duo from Orange Mound, the home of Melrose High School, electrified the fan bases in Memphis, Tennessee and became a catalyst for cementing the races in Memphis, Tennessee. This cemented fan base transformed Memphis State and the city of Memphis. Larry Finch and Ronnie Robinson formed the nucleus of a winning basketball team and a winning tradition at Memphis State University.

Success on the hardwood whetted the fan appetite for a better football program. To comply with fan demands, the University officials strategically met with Black community leaders seeking ways to improve their recruiting efforts for Black football players. In 1971, Pete Mitchell, the legendary football coach at Melrose High School, was hired as an assistant football coach at Memphis State University. Pete Mitchell played a major role in recruiting and in the development of

*Pete Mitchell*

high school football players. In addition to coaching assignments, he was a scout and recruiter of Black football players in the Mid-South. Pete Mitchell's success was unprecedented.

For years, the Memphis State Basketball program carried the economic weight of the entire athletic program, including football. The fan base was relentless in its demands for a top-notch football program at the University. Therefore, in pursuit of a top-notch football program the University hired proven coaches, recruited top football players, regardless of race, and made a financial commitment to the program. In the year 2010, the investments began to produce dividends. Coach Justin Fuente was hired and in 2014 led the Tigers to a 10 and 3 record and a national ranking. With that accomplishment, the University of Memphis had achieved the immediate goal of developing  a successful football program.

In 2015, the Virginia Tech University came knocking at the University of Memphis' football door courting Coach Fuente to join Virginia Tech as its head football coach. Fuente accepted the position at Virginia Tech and left a football coaching vacancy at the University of Memphis. The University then hired Mike Norvell  from Arizona State as the next University of Memphis football coach.

*Mike Norvell*

The winning tradition that began under Coach Justin Fuente continued under the explosive, pass-oriented offense coaching style of coach Mike Norvell.

In his first year, the tigers finished the season with an  8 and 5 record. At the end of coach Norvell's third year, the Tigers were nationally ranked with a 12 and 1 record and were champions of the American Athletic Conference. The AAC championship win led to the Tigers being invited to the Annual 2019 Cotton Bowl Game to play Penn State University. Shortly after being selected to play in the Cotton Bowl, Mike Norvell resigned as coach at the University of Memphis and accepted the head coaching  position at Florida State University.

As the seasons changed from football to basketball, Tiger fans were a buzz over the potential of a deep tournament run by another hometown

*Penny Haraway*

hoop star, Penny Hardaway. It is appropriate that Hardaway, who was coached by Larry Finch, is now the head coach for the Tiger's basketball team. Sports continue to bring this city together.

To ease the pain of Mike Norvell's departure, one should consider the wisdom of James Arthur Gray, Sr, now deceased teacher, and farmer from Jagoe, Mississippi, "Every time a bee extracts nectar from a flower, that bee makes a deposit for the next flower." The deposits for greatness and grandeur at the University of Memphis football and basketball programs have been left by people like Bobby 'Bingo' Smith, Herb Hillard, Larry Finch, and Coach Gene Bartow, who coached Larry Finch, Coach Larry Finch, and Coach Mike Norvell. Winning sure is sweet!

~ ~ ~ ~ ~

# LET THE PLANNING BEGIN

Venturing into 'the next 200 years of Soul' each Memphian should conduct the one question of self-examination, 'What role am I going to play?' The Work continues in the development of Downtown Memphis. This work is exemplified by the One Beale Development Project - a two-tower structure that will accentuate the city skyline, as well as provide retail space, apartments, and underground parking; after a long-awaited renovation, the Grand Central Railroad Station Project is now complete; the Medical District is expanding being led by the innovative and cutting-edge research of St. Jude Children's Hospital in the Historic Pinch District; and Methodist University Hospital expansion which is reflective of their dedication to meet the needs of an Urban Center. Also, the FedEx Forum is now an established venue for entertainment, collegiate and

*Grand Central Station*

professional sports. The River Front is alive and well and there is highly anticipated and renewed interest in the Beale Street Landing project.

*St. Jude Children's Hospital*

The Henry Turley Revolution continues in residential development in the Downtown Memphis area, especially on the Bluff. Renovation of Public Housing, that began under historic Mayor Dr. W. W. Herenton, continues under the visionary Mayor Jim Strickland and the capable leadership of Paul Young.

*Willie W. Herenton*

In addition, Archie Willis III, and the Church of God in Christ have collaborated with city government and the United States Department of Housing and Urban Development to provide upscale homes and apartments in a once blighted area of downtown Memphis. Lastly, but certainly not the least, Beale Street is jumping!

On October 3, 2019, his vision resonated with the citizens of Memphis that Jim Strickland was given a mandate to serve. He was reelected  for a second term as Mayor of Memphis with 62% of the vote. This vision included city funding for pre-K education, a Young Man University, designed to reduce recidivism among young men and women caught in the criminal justice system, and he courageously led the legal battle with County Commissioner Attorney Van Turner to remove the Confederate statues and symbols from the Memphis landscape.  He further ingratiated himself to the voting population when he made $50,000 tax free grants  available to the surviving members of the 1968 Sanitation Strike!

*Lee Harris*

County Mayor Lee Harris, elected in 2018, is casting his vision for a progressive and more responsible Shelby County government. Mayor Harris has made it known that his policy and programs will be driven by his compassion for the least, the lost, and the last. Memphis City Council is prepared for the future with a powerful new coalition led by five professional Black women. With Mark Billingsley and Eddie Jones as leaders of the County Commission, they are poised to work with Mayors Strickland and Harris to eradicate poverty, improve education, expand mass transit, and increase the number of minority contractors with city and county governments.

*Joris Ray*

*Jarl T. Young*

Dr. Joris Ray, former superintendent of Shelby County Schools, led with a committed resolve to enhance the educational experience of our children. He resolved to make the educational experiences and curriculum, student centered, and student focused in Shelby County Schools. He made a special commitment to saving young Black boys from the vicious cycle of poverty, crime, and subsequent low achievement.

Jarl T. Young, former CEO of Memphis Light Gas and Water Utility company, faced challenges during his tenure but also had some exciting alternatives. The long-standing marriage with TVA (Tennessee Valley Authority) must be revisited. The infrastructure of Memphis Light Gas and Water, for the delivery of services, must be updated.

Poverty in our city is the pressing issue for moving forward. To have 26.9 percent of our citizens living in poverty is totally unacceptable. Memphis now has the dubious distinction of leading the nation as the poorest Metropolitan statistical area. We can and we must alleviate poverty and improve life in this great city of Memphis.

The Chamber of Commerce, led by Willie Gregory, Richard Smith and Beverly Robertson, was the engine of flight to Memphis progress. This body of diverse and talented men and women were responsible for some 15 billion

*Beverly Robertson*

dollars of development in our city. By every diagnostic evaluation of urban centers, this was a healthy sign. We can and we must build on this momentum by including advocacy for entrepreneurial initiatives in poverty pockets of Memphis. Instead of jobs only, the Chamber of Commerce must encourage small business development and organize

*Willie Gregory*

*Richard Smith*

mentoring programs for small business owners. This innovative initiative must be led by corporate Memphis in partnership with the City and County Government.

The unfinished business of the Chamber of Commerce consists of building a memorial to the thousands of Black nurses, Black soldiers, and Black city workers who preserved, protected, and patrolled the streets of Memphis during the 1878 Yellow fever epidemic. This Yellow fever epidemic overwhelmingly affected the White population with 25,000 Whites fleeing the city when the epidemic was announced. Those Blacks who remained, making up 70% of the population after the fever struck and after Whites fled, were responsible for managing and distributing medical supplies, food, and general supplies that poured in from all over the nation.

*The 1878 Memphis Yellow Fever Epidemic Marker*

Blacks remained to serve the sick, bury the dead, and protect the property of others at the risk of losing their own lives. As a matter of 'poetic justice,' the ideal site for an overdue memorial to these courageous Black men and Black women would be the former site of the Nathan Bedford Forrest statue on Union Avenue in the medical district.

Robertson Topp deserves a street named in his honor as the founder of South Memphis, incorporated on January 6, 1846. The street that evolved as the major thoroughfare of South Memphis needed a name. His associates suggested that this main thoroughfare of South Memphis should be named Topp Avenue. His modesty, however, caused him to refuse that honor and he subsequently named that main thoroughfare Beale Avenue in honor of Edward F. Beale, a Mexican American war hero.

*Ed Beale*

# SELECTED BIBLIOGRAPHY

Babb, John. *Voices of the Dead*. Humble, TX: Dinbat Publishing, 2019.

Bond, Beverly G., and Janann Sherman. *Beale Street*. Charleston, SC: Arcadian Publishers, 2003.

Bond, Beverly G., and Janann Sherman. *Memphis in Black and White*. Charleston, SC: Arcadian Publishers, 2003.

Branston, John. *Rowdy Memphis: The South Unscripted*. Nashville, TN: Cold Tree Press, 2004.

Church, Annette, and Roberta Church. *The Robert R. Churches of Memphis*. Ann Arbor, MI: Edwards Brothers, 1974.

Church, Robert, and Ronald Walter. *Nineteenth Century Memphis Families of Color, 1850-1900*. Murdock Printing Company, 1987.

Devi, Debra. *The Language of the Blues: From Alchrub to Zuzu*. Billboard Books, 2006.

Dickerson, James. *Going Back to Memphis: A Century of Blues, Rock'N'Roll and Glorious Soul*. New York, NY: Schirmer Books, 1996.

Guaralnick, Peter. *Sam Phillips: The Man Who Invented Rock'N'Roll*. New York, NY: Brown and Company, 2015.

Handy, W. C. *Father of the Blues*. New York, NY: DaCapo Press, 1941.

Harkins, John E. *Memphis Chronicles*. Charleston, SC: History Press, 2009.

Harkins, John E. *Metropolis of the American Nile*. Oxford, MS: Guild Bindery Press, 1982.

Jones, LeRoi (Amiri Baraka). *Blues People*. New York, NY: Harper Collins Publishers, 2002.

Lauterbach, Preston. *Beale Street Dynasty*. New York, NY: W.W. Norton and Company, 2015.

Lauterbach, Preston. *Bluff City*. New York, NY: W.W. Norton and Company, 2019.

Lee, George W. *Beale Street, Where the Blues Began*. New York, NY: Ballou, 1934.

Mynbeer Nasser. *Upright Bass: The Musical Life and Legacy of Jami Nasser*. Lexington, KY: Vertical Visions Press, 2019.

Ranichelson, Richard M. *Beale Street Talks*. Arcadian Records, 1994.

Sanford, Otis. *From Boss Crump to King Willie*. Knoxville, TN, 2017.

Waltz Dawson. "Beale Street: Memphis Razed Blues Landmark." *Rolling Stone*, no. 140, August 1973, p. 21.

Weeks, Linton. *Memphis: A Folk History*. Little Rock, AR: Parkhurst Publishers, 1982.

Willis, Miriam De Costa. *Black Memphis Landmarks*. Jonesboro, AR: GrantHouse Publishers, 2010.

# About the Author

Dr. L. LaSimba M. Gray, Jr is the Pastor Emeritus of the Historic New Sardis Baptist Church in Germantown, Tennessee.  He served as Senior Pastor of New Sardis Baptist Church for 25 years, but celebrates 50 years of preaching.  In his prophetic ministry, he served as president of the Memphis satellite of Operation PUSH and served on the Tennessee Human Rights Commission under three Governors.

Dr. Gray is a graduate of Hamilton High School in Memphis, Tennessee. He earned a Bachelor of Science degree from Lane College in Jackson, Tennessee, in 1968.  His postgraduate education includes a Master's degree in Education from the University of Memphis, as well as a Master of Divinity degree and a Doctor of Ministry degree from the Memphis Theological Seminary.

Dr. Gray was nurtured in the Christian faith by loving, devoted Christian parents, the Reverend Leo M. Gray, Sr. and Mrs. Corine Olivia Gray.  He was baptized at the Middle Baptist Church in Memphis, Tennessee. It was at the Middle Baptist Church that the author was introduced to prophetic ministry. The Reverend E. W. Williamson, an activist in the Civil Rights Movement, ran for election to the Memphis City School Board, when it was not popular, nor safe, to do so. Dr. Benjamin Lawson Hooks served as the author's role model in the ministry for more than 50 years.

The author is married to the former Carol A. Sanders.  Together they have three daughters: Angelique Gray, an MBA Graphic Artist in Memphis; Dr. Leah Gray, an Optometrist in Memphis; and Attorney Memorie K. White of Nashville, Tennessee.

In 1990, the author organized a group of activists and filed a federal lawsuit challenging the runoff provision of city elections in Memphis. The federal court ruled, without a trial, that the runoff was unconstitutional. This ruling made it possible for Dr. W. W. Herenton to be elected as the first African American Mayor of the city of Memphis.

On December 5, 1999, the Shelby County Commission renamed a major section of Holmes Road in Memphis, "The Dr. L. LaSimba M. Gray, Jr. Road," in honor of the author's long tenure of service in Shelby County.

Dr. Gray previously served as the treasurer of the *New Tri-State Defender* Newspaper and as a Director for the Tri-State Bank of Memphis. He will be appointed the President of the Southern Christian Leadership Conference in fall of 2025.

# ALSO BY THE AUTHOR

## DR. L. LASIMBA GRAY, JR.

### *Out of Bounds: The History of African Americans and Golf in Memphis*

Out of Bounds: The History of African Americans and Golf in Memphis by Dr. LaSimba M. Gray explores the significant yet often overlooked role of African Americans in Memphis's golf scene, linking it to the broader Civil Rights Movement. The book highlights how golf served as a platform for challenging racial segregation and showcases the experiences of black golfers who faced systemic racism. Through personal stories and historical analysis, it honors the pioneers of the sport and illustrates golf's impact on social and political changes in Memphis, making it relevant to both golf enthusiasts and those interested in civil rights.

### *Available from*

### *and other online retailers.*